A CASUAL CONQUEST

A young man starts his first job in a distant colony – at the headquarters of the Honourable West Europa Company in Antwerp. He comes from Japan, in an 'alternative history' scenario in which Eighteenth Century Europe is strongly reminiscent of South Asia in the dying years of the Mughal Empire. Soon he is accompanying his boss on a mission to Hamburg, where he listens to the itinerant Mozart Minstrels and is seduced by the Duchess of Holstein (who in 'real time' would have been Catherine the Great).

His next journey takes him to the Shantungese colony of Britain, where he sees an altarpiece painted by Gainsborough and helps a young runaway nun escape to Antwerp. At a Council meeting he hears his bosses debate whether a trading company ought to take responsibility for governing failed states. Before long he is sent to observe a war between ambitious rulers of petty principalities; and he meets a famous native poet and philosopher. Soon he begins to miss the British girl he left in Antwerp, and wonders if she will welcome his return.

A Casual Conquest

Derek Walker

ISBN 978-1-4092-0340-7

Typesetting and design by Christine Price

Published 2008 by Derek Walker

Dorset Square, London NW1

Distribution at www.lulu.com

ABOUT THE AUTHOR

DEREK WALKER was born and grew up in Northern Ireland. He graduated at the London School of Economics and since then has continued to live in London. For ten years he worked as a journalist, and in 1966 became Education Officer of the newly-formed Voluntary Committee on Overseas Aid and Development. When VCOAD was dissolved in 1977 he became Director of the Centre for World Development Education (later renamed Worldaware) which took over its educational work. In 1997 he was appointed OBE. Since retiring from Worldaware in 2000 he has published five novels (see end pages).

AD 1777 PART OF NORTHERN EUROPA
Nominal frontier of the 'Janissary Empire'
Other frontiers
HAMBURG
DUCHY OF MECKLENBURG
Bremen
DUCHY OF HOLSTEIN
DUCHY OF BRUNSWICK
DUCHY OF BRANDENBURG
BERLIN
Enschede
Minden
BRUNSWICK
Hameln
Hildesheim
Magdeburg
WITTENBERG
Goslar
PASHALIK OF THE NETHERLANDS
Administered by the Honourable West Europa Company
ANTWERP
PASHALIK OF LORRAINE
Cologne
Leipzig
DUCHY OF SAXONY
PASHALIK OF FRANCONIA
FRANKFURT
DUCHY OF NORMANDY
DOMAIN OF THE SULTAN
DUCHY OF BOHEMIA

CHAPTER 1

For a brief moment the morning sunlight blinded us as we came up on deck, and then simultaneously Takahashi and I saw it – a long, white streak on the larboard horizon.

"Land!" he exclaimed. "But it's on the wrong side of the ship. Europa should be on the right-hand side."

"It must be the island of Britain," I said. The night before, in eager anticipation of arriving at our destination, I had studied the map before climbing into my hammock, and so I knew that we would have to pass through a narrow strait in order to reach the port of Antwerp and the end of our seven-month voyage.

"Do you remember that bit in *Lands of the Setting Sun*, where it said the women on that island have beautiful, long yellow hair and pink and white skin?" asked Takahashi. As schoolboys we had both been given the same book about the wonders of the Far West, and it had probably played some small part in the decisions made by both of us to enter the service of the Honourable West Europa Company. Takahashi was taking up a commission in the Company's Walloon Regiment of Native Infantry – principally because it was more affordable to his father than a commission in the Imperial Army would have been. Through my Uncle Hiriomi, who had joined the Company's Board of Directors in Edo after twenty-two years' service in Europa, I had obtained the lowly post of 'Writer'. But I knew that I was not going to be assigned to mundane clerkly duties, for Uncle Hiriomi had also arranged for me to become secretary to his old friend, Shinroku Okada, who was the Senior Factor assisting the Governor-General with the Company's external relations in Europa. So it was not just the prospect of stepping on to dry land after seven months of shipboard privations (albeit in the comparative luxury of a three-master West Europaman) that was now filling me with eager anticipation.

"Yes, but I can't remember it saying anything about the women in the Netherlands Province," I replied. "They're the ones we need to be interested in."

"They're probably all locked up in harems."

"It's only the Muslims who do that. The Netherlanders mostly belong to the Christian religion, apart from the big landowners and some of the officials, I think."

"I bet the Christians keep their daughters locked up, too. Of course, the place where the fellows in my regiment come from might be different. It's in the south of the province. They speak a different language from the natives around Antwerp. I've not been making much progress with it. The book doesn't really give you much idea how to pronounce the words and I can't get them into my head."

"I know. I've had the same trouble with Turkish. The Supercargo is the only man on the ship who speaks it, and he's given me a bit of help, but I still can't get the hang of it."

"It's all right for you," he said glumly. "You'll be dealing mainly with the bigwigs, and they probably talk some Japanese. My fellows will all be peasants. And if I ever get transferred to a Hollander regiment I'll have to start all over again. They speak something completely different. With all these different languages it's no wonder they can't get themselves organized."

"That doesn't seem to have hindered us much in East Asia – having a lot of different languages," I objected. "And it must be a help that all the educated people in the Christian races are able to talk to each other in the Latin language. I suppose it's a bit like the way we used in the old days to make more use of Mandarin."

"I always hated learning Mandarin at school. But from what I've heard there aren't very many educated people; so the Latin you've been learning might not be much use to you. This language business is what I like least about coming here. I wish we could make them all learn Japanese."

"I can't see the *Hakata*," I said, interrupting him. "Where do you think she's got to?" I had been idly scanning our convoy, which was looking its most impressive under full sail with a strong following breeze, and had noted the absence of one of the escorting frigates, usually to be seen fussing around like a hen with over-sized chickens. (I suppose I thought 'hen' rather than 'duck' because I was essentially still a landlubber.)

"Didn't you know? She left us yesterday for Bordeaux," Takahashi replied. "She's gone there to join the Atlantic Squadron.

But the *Sakai* is still with us. Look, you can just see her back there, keeping an eye on the stragglers, I suppose."

For several minutes we stood gazing at the irregular line of ships stretching to the south-west with the morning sun giving lustre to their weather-beaten sails. Then I said, "I'm going below to finish packing my gear. With any luck we should be ashore in time to get a decent meal before sunset. It'll be our first since the fresh food we took on at Promontory Town ran out."

"I can't wait to get my teeth into a piece of fresh pork with crispy crackling," said Takahashi.

Walking on dry land produced a slightly odd sensation next morning as I made my way to Okada's office in the Fort. My brain was still making adjustments for the roll of the ship. A native servant with short yellow hair, wearing a blue, Eastern-style uniform, led me upstairs. He appeared to understand Japanese but said nothing, merely giving me a deep bow as he ushered me into a high-ceilinged room with two tall windows overlooking the courtyard. At the far end, behind a large desk, sat a short, broad-shouldered man with grey hair and a deeply-lined face who rose to welcome me. Our exchange of greetings was much less formal than it would have been at home. My uncle had warned me to expect less formality, adding, however, that when he'd returned after twenty-two years' absence he'd been surprised to discover how much simpler manners in Japan had become since he was a boy.

When I had sat down in one of two large, Western-style chairs in front of his desk Okada said, "Shall we have some tea? Nothing elaborate, as you'll see, but the quality is good. As you probably know, it's one of the Company's principal imports here. The natives have really taken to it – those who can afford it." He rang a little brass bell that was sitting on his desk.

While we were awaiting the tea he gave me a rapid outline of how the administration was organized. The Governor-General was now, since the passing of the Regulatory Act four years ago, in control of all three of the Company's European territories, with the Governors in Bordeaux and Naples subordinate to him. Most of what Okada told me I already knew from the briefing I'd received at West Europa

House in Edo. But the practicalities of who did what, and how the trading activities were separated from the mushrooming responsibilities of government – or rather three governments – were new to me.

When the tea arrived it was brought by another novelty for my eyes – a woman. It had been a long time since I'd last been close to one, for the ship in which I travelled had carried no female passengers, although there had been several on board two other ships in the convoy. She was taller than the average Japanese woman, and she carried the large tray confidently, with uncovered forearms that looked quite muscular. A high-waisted, long brown dress obscured her figure, but it was evident that her bosom was bountiful by Eastern standards, and the light brown colour of her hair, gathered in a large bun at the nape of her neck, was entirely new to me. When she had poured the tea into small, flower-patterned cups that must have come from Japan, she curtsied with just the hint of a smile on her broad, fair-skinned face.

"Thank you, Juliana," said Okada; and I was impressed, and encouraged, by this politeness shown to a servant.

Tea in hand, he then looked at me and enquired, "Did you leave your uncle in good health?"

"Yes, sir," I replied. "He was very well when we parted in Edo."

"Did he ever tell you that he saved my life at Passchendaele?"

"No, sir. He never even told me he was at Passchendaele. I didn't know he'd been in the army."

"He wasn't, nor was I. But before Passchendaele things were very bad. The Pasha of the Netherlands had mustered an army of thirty thousand or more and the Company had only some two and a half thousand men. So they raised a small battalion of 'volunteers' – though I don't recall we were given any choice in the matter – made up of all the able-bodied Japanese men working in the factory, here in Antwerp, and some sailors from the ships in the harbour. Your uncle and I were in the ranks, and we had a couple of weeks to learn how to use our muskets and bayonets before we marched off to meet the Pasha's horde. What happened after that I'm sure you've heard or read."

Like every other Japanese schoolboy I had, indeed, been told about that famous victory, which was won, as it happened, in the year that I was born. "I have indeed, sir," I said, "But how did my uncle come to save your life?"

"Our small battalion was on the left flank and early in the battle we were attacked by a regiment of Berber mercenaries. They came at us at a great rate – high on hashish, I expect – and though we decimated them with a couple of volleys they kept on coming. But now their line was pretty ragged and one big fellow who was wearing a spiked helmet under his turban was a few paces ahead of the rest and coming straight at me. I thrust at him but he caught my bayonet on the little round shield he was carrying. Now we'd been taught in bayonet practice that every man should thrust to his right at the unprotected side of the enemy attacking his neighbour, but that tactic only works if every man plays his part. The man on my left must have been frightened out of his wits by this huge, black-faced savage waving a sword, and instead of thrusting he turned away. Your uncle was the man on my right and he saw out of the corner of his eye what was happening. It was a split second decision for him. He thrust to his left and caught the big fellow through the cheek with the point of his bayonet just as his sword was sweeping down on me. It was enough to put the man off his stroke and the blade only grazed my shoulder. Then the rest of them were on top of us, but our second rank had closed up and were thrusting at them over our shoulders. We held the line, and because they were unsupported the Walloon battalion on our right was able to blast them with a couple of volleys that sent them scampering back to their own line – those that were still able to.

"That was my only experience of soldiering, and for your uncle, too, I think. But every day when I'm bathing I see that scar and I remember him."

As he told the story I imagined myself in his predicament and hoped fervently that I would never have to take my place in a line of battle. If I did, would I be able to muster the courage that he and Uncle Hiriomi had shown or would I, like the man on his left, try to run away? The thought disturbed me, and several seconds elapsed before I responded to the story, saying, "Thank you for telling me, sir. I shall think differently of my uncle in the future."

Okada nodded solemnly. "We need more men like him in the Company. I hope you're going to be one of them."

"I shall try hard to follow his example, with your help, sir."

"See that you do. I hope you made use of the voyage to improve your command of the Latin language."

"I did, sir, but I had little opportunity to practise speaking it because there was no one on the ship proficient in the language."

"Well, you will very soon have the opportunity to hear a great deal of it – I hope. The day after tomorrow we go travelling, and the people we'll be dealing with have a vernacular called German, of which I have little knowledge. We'll be taking an interpreter, of course, but I hope that the really important people will be sufficiently fluent in Latin to make private conversations a possibility. At the formal meetings I will, of course, require you to take a note of what is said. Not every word," he added, as my face may have betrayed the alarm that I felt, "for that would not be possible. What I shall require is an accurate summary of every significant statement that is made. On the journey I will give you some practice.

"But we'll talk more about the practicalities later. Now, I want to make sure that you understand the essential facts about this place and the people we shall be dealing with. Did they give you any instruction in the politics of the sub-continent at West Europa House?"

"No, sir; but they gave me the books by Arima and Oishi to read on the voyage. I found them very interesting, but Oishi doesn't have very much to say about the political situation."

"I met the fellow about ten years ago, when he was on his travels. No doubt he's a good scholar, but he's not a practical man. The trouble with books like that is they're out of date almost before they're printed. We live here in a rapidly changing scene, and there is a huge gap between appearances and reality. This map is a very good example of it."

He got up and stood beside the huge map on the wall behind his desk, gesturing to me with one hand to remain seated as, impelled by good manners, I began to rise from my chair. The map covered a larger area than the one in Arima's *History and Religions of Europa*, with which I had familiarised myself. From north to south it reached from the top of the British island down to the northern coast of Africa.

Okada picked up a ruler from his desk to use as a pointer and began my instruction. "This heavy red line purports to represent the frontiers of the Empire of Europa – or 'the Janissary Empire', as it's popularly known. Total fiction, of course. That's where the frontiers were about seventy years ago, when Sultan Mustafa died. He was the last strong ruler and after his death three of his sons fought each other for the succession, starting a continuing process of disintegration, as I'm sure you know. There had been some fragmentation before, in the previous century, after the death of Sultan Ahmed; but Mustafa had pulled it all together again, very ruthlessly, and had even extended the territory controlled from Augsburg.

"You'll have read Arima's account of the numerous wars, invasions and rebellions that took place over the three decades before Ibrahim was acknowledged as Sultan. By that time all the outlying provinces were either independent or virtually autonomous. Then came the invasion by the Magyars. For over a century they had formed a buffer kingdom between the Empire and the Ottoman territories to the south-east. You will recall that it was originally the Ottomans who took over Europa three centuries ago, after the final departure of the Mongols. And then, about seventy years later, their crack troops, the Janissaries, rebelled and decided to run the sub-continent for their own benefit. By playing Augsburg and Istanbul off against each other the Magyars managed to carve out a sizeable kingdom for themselves here" – he pointed to the right of the map – "between the two Muslim empires.

"Anyhow, that Magyar invasion was only a temporary incursion. Once they'd sacked Augsburg they went home again, taking a huge amount of plunder and emptying the Sultan's treasure, so that he had no money left to pay his troops. The immediate result was that many of the German-speaking Christians in the eastern part of the Empire" – he swept the tip of the ruler downward in an arc, from the Baltic to the Adriatic – "were able to secure their independence under local warlords, known as the German Dukes. There are half-a-dozen of them, perpetually at each other's throats. But more about them later, because you'll be meeting some of them very shortly.

"With the Sultan's authority in ruins it wasn't long before most of his Christian subjects in the Italian peninsula managed to break free, under a variety of different rulers. Again, I'll come back to them later, because the Company's very profitable factory at Naples sits in the midst of them.

"In the west there were also a succession of revolts around that time, but the Christian natives have finally secured their independence in only two areas, the Duchies of Brittany and Normandy. The former has its own language, but in Normandy they speak French, which is the language of most of the western region and also, of course, of the Walloons who live in the south of this province.

"However, the remaining provinces of the Empire, shown on this map inside the red frontier line, are a fiction too. Their governors, called 'pashas', may find it convenient to pay lip-service to the Sultan in Augsburg, but in practice they have become independent rulers of their own little kingdoms. You can see here they follow a kind of arc from east to west." Again using the ruler, he pointed out the provinces. "Down on the Adriatic coast you have Venetia; and then, over the mountains, Bavaria, the only province where the Sultan's writ still runs, because that's where the imperial capital, Augsburg, is situated.

"Then to the north and west you have Franconia and Swabia, and beyond them Lorraine and Burgundy. Farther west are the Pashaliks of Champagne and Anjou, here to the south of the Christian Duchies. South of that is an area of particular importance to the Company, of course. Twelve years ago our Governor in Bordeaux was given effective control of the hinterland to the north of the city, known as Guyenne, after the Pasha's two sons had both been killed in a battle for the succession. To the north-east of that, here in the centre of the region" – he tapped on the map with the ruler – "a general who quarrelled with Sultan Mustafa the Second some twenty years ago carved out a domain for himself which he calls the Emirate of Touraine. But more importantly, this large territory to the south and east is ruled by a very dangerous character who gives himself the grandiose title of 'Sultan of Aquitaine'. We've had trouble with him in the past and I'm sure it won't be long before he troubles us again."

"And to the south of the mountains, the Pyrenees, has anything changed there?" I asked.

"The Iberian Peninsular? No, it remains comparatively peaceful – and backward. It's never been part of the Janissary Empire, of course. As you can see, there are five little Christian kingdoms in the north and west, and three Muslim emirates in the south. The Shantungese have a factory on the west coast, at a place called Oporto. They moved there after the great earthquake wiped out their first factory in Lisbon. That was the year before I arrived in Europa. I can remember people pointing out to me as we sailed into Antwerp the wreckage of ships that were destroyed even as far north as here by the tsunami that followed it.

"But that's enough geography for the moment. You have clearly done your homework. Although you will not have time to settle in before we begin our journey, I will now introduce you to the people and the procedures with which you will be working in this establishment."

We then set out on a rapid tour of the Company's offices that left me with a head full of faces and names that I quickly resolved I must try to set down on a sheet of paper. I feared that when I was next required to seek out one of them I might make a fool of myself by addressing a Senior Factor with the name of a junior apprentice. However, I was reassured when, at the end of the tour, we arrived back at a small office next to Okada's which I was to share with a native clerk named Kees Zalm. He was a Hollander and his work, he told me, consisted of translating documents from Japanese into Latin or his native language, Dutch, or sometimes into French, in which he was also fluent. I was greatly impressed by his skill, for he conversed easily with me in Japanese; and I soon formed a judgement that he was a man I would be able to trust.

Kees appeared to be some three or four years older than myself. (I subsequently discovered that the age gap was actually five years.) When Okada had left us I very quickly indicated by the manner in which I addressed him that I had no intention of treating him as a subordinate, even though technically that was his status. Immediately he became less formal, and before long we were telling each other about our families.

His father had been a fish merchant whose business had been destroyed when the Pasha had confiscated all his money – and his horse and cart – in 'taxation' to pay for the army he raised before the Battle of Passchendaele. Now his father was working for the Company as a book-keeper, and had responsibility for recording all the taxes sent to Antwerp by the Company's Collectors throughout the province. He himself had been educated in a Company school for native boys thought clever enough to become useful employees. Although he was unmarried (something he confirmed was unusual at his age) he hoped by next year to have saved enough money to marry

Annemarie, the daughter of a man who also worked for the Company, and provide her with a comfortable home.

I told him about my school and the university in Sendai, where I had spent three happy, if not very profitable, years and, of course, about my Uncle Hiriomi – which greatly impressed him. I asked him about Mr Okada and was reassured to learn that Kees had found him a very fair employer and a man of great ability, much respected by his colleagues and by the Governor-General. He knew that I would shortly be accompanying Okada on his next journey, and greatly regretted that he would not be coming too, because he wasn't a German-speaker. However, he said he was a good friend of Okada's manservant, Wim Dijkstal, and would ask him to be helpful to me on the journey.

When it was time to leave the office and return to my living quarters at the end of the afternoon I already felt part of this strange organization that was buzzing around me like a beehive. Depending on whom I was talking to, it took the shape of either a government or a shipping line or a military headquarters or a trading company. For the moment my own work seemed to be firmly located in its governmental functions, as assistant to its chief diplomat. But just before the end of the day Okada told me to familiarize myself with a document we would be taking on our journey. It was a draft agreement exempting from tariffs the codfish being brought to Europa by the Company's new North Atlantic fishing fleet. I could see there were no clear boundaries between the different functions.

But as Kees closed the office door behind us hunger quickly emptied my mind of thoughts about work, and I began to speculate on what kind of food might be on offer at the evening meal.

CHAPTER 2

I had not expected to be shipboard again so soon after my arrival in Europa, and I didn't enjoy the short voyage from Antwerp to Hamburg, capital of the Duchy of Holstein. Five centuries ago, before the Mongol invasion, it had been a prosperous independent city, Okada told me when he briefed me for the journey. Now, after some fifty years of freedom from the Sultan's rule, it was just beginning to emerge as a commercial centre, and he was anxious to ensure that the Company would have a dominant share of its trade, and of Holstein's three other ports, Emden, Bremen and Lubeck. As we finally approached the city, having navigated the interminable estuary of the River Elbe, I was unimpressed by the primitive wooden quays along the river-bank and the straggle of weather-beaten small ships which were moored alongside them. I remembered reading that for more than a century the Janissary Sultans had forbidden their subjects on the northern coasts to build any vessels larger than fishing-boats, and wondered if they had lost whatever skills they might originally have possessed.

"I expect the Duchess will send a reception party to greet us," said Okada, standing beside me on the quarterdeck. "They know we're coming, and they're bound to have seen our arrival from the castle." He gestured towards a cluster of grey towers rising beyond the roofs of the city, about a mile away.

"Will we have to walk there?" I asked, thinking about what kind of footwear I needed.

"Last time I came she sent her own coach to meet me – a rather splendid vehicle with gilding round the windows but pretty primitive suspension. And there was what looked like a scrubbed-down farmcart to convey the luggage. Wim had a rickety ride in it over the cobbles. But at least they do have cobbles, unlike the streets in a lot of towns to the east of here."

Sure enough, within half-an-hour our escort had arrived. It was led by a very grand individual riding a white horse and wearing a long, plum-coloured velvet coat with an ermine collar and a high-crowned hat trimmed with an ostrich feather. He announced himself, in Latin, as Baron Karl von Rendsburg, High Chamberlain to Her Grace the Duchess Sophia Augusta Frederica, and welcomed us to Holstein in her name. Okada responded appropriately, and before long he and I were seated in the gilded coach, jolting over cobbled streets. Behind us Wim and a sergeant and corporal of the Marines rode in a large cart bearing our few items of luggage. We were accompanied by six Holstein troopers clad in bright steel cuirasses and helmets, mounted on magnificent black horses, finer than any I had ever seen in Japan. (Sometime later Okada told me the Company was shipping back several young stallions to set up a stud-farm near Omiya.)

At the castle we were conducted by the Chamberlain to a grim-looking tower in which we were to be quartered. The rooms were comfortably furnished, with Asian rugs on the floors and heavy curtains at the windows, and in each bedroom – Okada's and mine – there was a huge four-poster bed with embroidered curtains. Rendsburg informed us that the Duchess would be graciously pleased to receive us at midday, and then withdrew, leaving a tall, yellow-haired servant who spoke little Japanese to attend to our needs.

While we were waiting for someone to fetch us to the presence of the Duchess Okada told me more about this unusual woman, a female ruler in her own right. By all accounts her husband, to whom she was married at the age of fifteen, had been little better than an idiot. When his father died, his strong-minded mother had become the effective ruler, keeping him firmly in order. But when she died, two years later, the young man had begun to run amok, declaring what could have been a disastrous war on the neighbouring Kingdom of Scandinavia. At that point some of the leading military men had forcibly removed him from office on the grounds of insanity, and acclaimed Sophia as the new ruler. Shortly afterwards he had died in mysterious circumstances.

In the fifteen years that had elapsed since those events, said Okada, Duchess Sophia had shown herself to be a remarkably able ruler. She had first led the country in a successful defensive war against neighbouring rulers who had tried to question the doubtful succession for their own ends; and since then she had begun to modernize the wretchedly poor region over which she presided.

Okada went on to tell me that the Duchess had one son, Otto, who was born the year before her husband's death. Rumour had it that the boy's father was actually one of the men who had led the coup, but that had never been confirmed. However, it was well known that the Duchess had had more than one lover, her most recent favourite having died tragically in a shipwreck only a few months ago. Needless to say, I was now eager to see this remarkable woman.

An officer accoutred in a gilded version of the uniform worn by the troopers of the mounted escort came to conduct us to our reception. He led us downstairs and across the courtyard to a large, single-storey stone building with high, narrow windows. It looked newer than the rest of the castle's structures and when we entered I saw that the timbers of the lofty ceiling were comparatively fresh. I guessed that it must have been constructed as a place in which to hold banquets and other grand events. At one end of the hall some fifty people were clustered around a dais on which the Duchess was enthroned.

"This is going to be just an opportunity to show us off to the local bigwigs," Okada said quietly, as we turned to approach the dais. "The serious talking will be done later, in private."

I dropped behind him as we walked down the centre of the hall, conscious that every eye was turned on us. To my surprise, the Duchess stood up as we approached. She was nearly my own height, which would have been moderately tall for a Japanese woman, and she held herself very erect. Her blue dress was cut to reveal the whole of her slender neck, and her glossy, black hair was uncovered, apart from a small tiara which twinkled with what may have been diamonds as she stepped forward into a shaft of sunlight from one of the tall windows. I was struck by the redness of her cheeks; but what really caught my attention as we arrived at the edge of the dais was the bright blue of her eyes, and their long, black lashes.

Okada bowed low from the waist and I imitated him. The Duchess smiled and began to address us in Latin, loudly and clearly so that everyone could hear her. She welcomed us cordially and said how greatly she valued the Honourable West Europa Company. It was a relationship which she hoped would continue to ensure the peace, prosperity and safety of those whom it brought together in amity. She also expressed pleasure at being able to extend her hospitality for a second time to the distinguished representative of the Governor-General, who had done so much to create good understanding between the two domains. And her cordial welcome extended also to his youthful companion, she added, with a glance from her bright blue eyes that scanned me from head to toe – and caused me to recollect that I'd forgotten to polish my boots.

Okada responded to her welcome in similar vein, assuring her of the Governor-General's continued respect and admiration. He then stepped forward and proffered a gift, a wooden casket decorated with black lacquer and gold and silver foil. The Duchess received it, smiling, and handed it to a yellow-haired lady-in-waiting to open. When its contents were revealed she exclaimed in delight, taking out a necklace of amber beads and holding it against her bosom to be admired.

She then stepped down from the dais and, taking Okada by the elbow, led him towards the group on her right. I followed discreetly, and as the introductions began I tried hard to remember the names. A white-haired man in voluminous robes and a red skull cap was the Archbishop of Bremen, a high religious dignitary; and a yellow-bearded man wearing a long, straight, Western-type sword, who towered over us all, was Count Dietrich von Oldenburg commander of the Holstein army. Those two would be easy to remember.

When the introductions were completed the Duchess invited the guests to partake of refreshments from two long tables which had appeared at the far end of the hall while we were talking. Okada and myself she then led through a door to a small anteroom where a table was laid out with plates of food and tall jugs which presumably contained drink. An elderly man in a black gown and cap was standing by the table and bowed low when we entered. The Duchess introduced him as her confidential secretary; but for the first few minutes he took the role of footman and served the food and drink (a beer which I found not unpleasant).

The Duchess was clearly at ease with Okada, and it was not long before they had reached agreement about the importation of fish to Holstein, some of it destined to travel farther inland on the waterways of the Elbe and the Weser. I picked up from their conversation that fish had some religious significance for the natives, and so their demand for it was insatiable even when they lived far away from the sea. (Afterwards Okada explained that the Christians were forbidden to eat meat on the day of the week on which their god had once been killed, and on that day fish was used as a substitute. It sounded bizarre but he seemed to be certain of his facts.)

I sensed that this trading agreement, which was going to be formally signed and sealed on the following day, was not the only reason why Okada had travelled all the way to Hamburg. The

Duchess went on to talk about improving the lot of the peasants by reducing a tax on salt, and by requiring the landowners to provide schools in all the villages on their estates. "At present the only education most children receive is from the priests, who teach them to recite the Catechism" (the name for a statement of beliefs, I discovered) "and fill their heads with ridiculous stories about the saints. They need to be taught to read and write and count their numbers," she said. "I've told the aristocrats we shall all become a lot richer when more people have learned to read and write. And I'm well aware that some of them are not too proficient themselves."

Education continued for some time to be the topic of conversation, and I was asked to describe my experience at the University of Sendai. In response I talked about the changes that were exciting students, if not their professors, in our universities, and about the way that mathematics and the natural sciences were altering ideas about what needed to be learnt – even though I myself had followed a more traditional course of study. So I spoke enthusiastically of mingling with fellow-students who were learning about the new discoveries of the past hundred years that had so quickly expanded what we know about East Asia," I said. "Every year scholars are having to accept that some belief they've always held about the way things work was only a bad guess, and now there's a new answer that's been put to the test and shown to be true."

"Give me an example," said the Duchess, transfixing me with a glance from those strongly hypnotic blue eyes.

"Well… just before I left Japan I read in a journal about a pharmacist in Kirin – I'm sorry I can't remember his peculiar name – who has made an astonishing discovery about the air we breathe," I replied. "He has discovered by experiment that it's not a single substance, but can be separated into several different gases. One of them, which he calls 'burning air', seems to be the reason why it's possible to set things on fire. And his experiment shows that fire isn't something that exists as a separate 'element', like the ancient philosophers taught: it's a process, not a substance."

The Duchess pursed her lips and continued to fix me with her gaze. "That's a very disturbing idea. Our ancient philosophers also taught that the universe is made up of four elements: earth, water, fire and air. Now it would seem that two of them don't really exist. But do these new ideas make any difference to the way that people do things in East Asia?" she asked.

"Oh yes, Your Grace," I replied. "I have seen this happening. My father owned a mill for spinning cotton thread, and he used the running water in a river to turn the wheels of the machinery. Then, three years ago, he heard about a new way to produce the power to turn wheels in machinery, by using steam that is produced continuously by burning coal to boil water. Now he has a much bigger mill, with spinning machines that work faster, and when I left home he was planning to build a second mill. Myself, I don't understand how they work, but my father says that before very long new ways will be found to use the power that steam engines can generate. But you need to have mathematics and very accurate measurements to make the engines work properly. If more people are taught those skills there will be more inventions."

"Measurements, measurements – you Easterners are always thinking about measuring," said the Duchess. "You have clocks in all your buildings and on your ships as well, I'm told. And you, young man, I expect you even have a little clock in your pocket."

"Yes, I have, Your Grace." I proudly displayed the watch my father gave me when I passed my final examinations. It had cost as much as he paid a mill-worker in a whole year, he told me.

Okada also looked at it with interest, commenting, "That's smaller than they used to make them when I got mine – but that would have been before you were born."

"You are wise to take such good care of time," the Duchess commented. "It's too precious to be wasted. I can't even get my people to come to dinner at the time when it's supposed to begin. Some arrive too early and some always come late. But then they have no clocks. I think I should put one in some high place in the city, where everyone can see it. No doubt the Company could supply us with one, Mr Okada?"

"Yes, indeed, Your Grace. I believe a clockmaker we brought from Japan last year to do work for us is still in Antwerp. I'm sure he would be pleased to undertake work for you."

The Duchess smiled and gestured to her secretary to make a note. This reminded me that I also had a note-taking function, and I reached into my pocket for the paper tablet and pencil to record Okada's offer.

"Speaking of time," the Duchess went on, "it would appear to be running out for my neighbour, the Duke of Brunswick. I received news yesterday that Maximilian has caught the smallpox and is not expected to live."

Okada looked startled. "I was at sea yesterday. I suppose that's why the information didn't reach me," he said, sounding as if his ignorance of this event was a failing that needed to be excused. "There will be a difficult problem about the succession, will there not? He has no children."

"There will be a great struggle and we must be prepared." Her expression had become serious and intense. "He has a cousin, Caroline, who is married to Ferdinand, a cousin of Joseph of Hapsburg, who calls himself Archduke of Austria. But there's also a male descendent of Maximilian's great-uncle, a young man called Franz, who is married to a niece of Frederick, the Duke of Prussia. Since the title is supposed to descend in the male line he could be said to have the better claim. And he lives in Brunswick."

"That should also give him an advantage," Okada commented.

"Yes, but I understand he's not very popular with some of the nobility there," said the Duchess. "He seduced a few of their wives and escaped the consequences by invoking Maximilian's protection. And that also means he's not popular with the clergy. On the other hand, I think a lot of the nobility would be uneasy about Joseph of Austria's cousin becoming, in effect, their ruler. You know that Joseph has been putting around the notion that there should be a restoration of the Holy Roman Empire, so that we can all unite more effectively to recover the rest of the German lands from the Muslims? And it so happens that the last of the Holy Roman Emperors, who was killed in the Mongol invasion just about five hundred years ago, was one of his ancestors – a man called Rudolf. Guess who he thinks should be the new emperor?"

Seeing my look of bewilderment she went on, "I expect you haven't heard about the Holy Roman Empire, young man. It's ancient history, but it seems to be one of those ideas that keeps coming round in a cycle every time this continent starts to push back its barbarians. The first time around – I suppose it was about a thousand years ago – they were trying to imitate an empire that covered a large part of Europa for hundreds of years in the really ancient times. That empire began in the city of Rome, in Italy; and the strange thing is that we Germans were the one people in Europa who were never part of it. That time around, we were the barbarians who destroyed it; but hundreds of years later when we had become Christians and had got ourselves together in a kind of empire, 'Roman' was the name that we gave to it. Maybe we did that because Rome in those days was still the centre of the Christian religion. What do you think, Otto?"

The secretary looked up from his writing-tablet and considered for a moment before replying. "Your Grace is right, I am sure," he said. "There was at that time a pope and it was he who crowned the emperors. And of course the empire then extended from Germany through Italy."

"I've heard mention of these popes before," said Okada. "Were they the Chief Priests for all the Christians?"

"For all in Western Europa," the secretary replied. "The Greeks and the Slavs had their own arrangements, and they still do."

"But there is no pope now," said Okada. "What became of them?"

"The last of them was killed by the Mongols," said the Duchess. "His name was Urban…?"

"Urban the Fourth," the secretary interjected.

"… Urban the Fourth, and they put him in a sack and let their horses trample him to death. It seems they were a very superstitious people and they didn't want to be responsible for killing a holy man with their own hands; so they thought that by letting the horses do it they could avoid the responsibility. Later on attempts were made to elect a new pope, but they all ended badly. When the Turks came they allowed the Church still to have bishops because they could use them to communicate with the common people, and the Janissary sultans did the same. But now that a lot of Christian states are free from Muslim rule there has been talk of having a pope once again. The priests say they need somebody to lay down the law on what are the right beliefs and practices for the Church, because over the centuries people have begun to do things differently in different parts of the continent. It depended mainly on what individual bishops believed. The sultans would never allow all the bishops to get together because they were afraid they might stir up a rebellion. When some of them tried to hold a secret Church Council about a hundred years ago they had their heads cut off.

"You'll not be surprised to hear that Archduke Joseph is now talking very loudly about the need to have a pope," she went on, smiling conspiratorially at Okada. "And there is talk that one of his nephews, who happens to be a bishop, would be a very suitable candidate for the post."

"What does Frederick of Brandenburg think about this idea of having a new Holy Roman Empire?" Okada asked.

"Frederick would never want to have Joseph lording it over him as emperor, and he knows that's what it would amount to. But he also knows that if the Slavs were ever to cross the Oder it would need the strength of all the duchies together to resist them. At the moment he's on good terms with the Slav Emperor in Cracow, whose main interest just now is gaining ground from the Turks on his southern frontier. But that might not last for ever.

"What Frederick wants most is more territory, so that he can build up his army. He has a long frontier with Brunswick. For him it's an apple just waiting to be plucked; and now it looks as if the apple might be ripe."

Okada nodded his head. "Joseph, on the other hand, has no frontier with Brunswick," he said. "If the claim of his cousin's wife were to be resisted he would have to move through both Bohemia and Saxony in order to enforce it. Would their dukes be likely to support him?"

"They might, but for different reasons," the Duchess replied. "He might well try to bribe Albrecht of Saxony, by suggesting he could have Brandenburg – or the greater part of it – once they'd defeated Frederick. And Sigismund of Bohemia might be pleased to join in an alliance with Austria and Saxony, because one of these days he might need some support against his own subjects. More than half of them are not German, and if they've now stopped being afraid of the Muslims they might be getting restless. I hear that they're very religious but don't get along with their German bishops."

"So you think Joseph has put together some kind of alliance?" asked Okada.

"I think he will be starting to do it now, if he's heard about Maximilian's illness."

"And are there no other possible claimants to Brunswick?"

The Duchess looked steadily at Okada, as though weighing up whether or not to reply to his question. The secretary cleared his throat nervously. After a pause that probably lasted only thirty seconds, but seemed longer, she said, "There is one other person who could be said to have a claim, although at this moment not many people are aware of the fact. It is something that might be better to remain undisclosed until other possibilities have been… what should I say… exhausted?"

Okada smiled and nodded his head. "Exhausted is a very appropriate word," he agreed. "But is there really a third possible claimant?"

Glancing at the secretary, she replied, "Yes, there is. As well as the daughter who became the mother of Caroline, Maximilian's grandfather had a son. Unfortunately he wasn't married to the boy's mother, but he did acknowledge his paternity. It's on record. And when the boy grew up he married and had a daughter, Charlotte, who also married – at the age of sixteen – and became the mother of my late husband, just about nine months later."

She paused and looked steadily at Okada, who slowly nodded his head three times before saying, "So your son, Otto, is a direct descendent of the duke who liberated Brunswick from the Sultan. The lawyers might argue about legitimacy, but some of the barons in Brunswick might take a different view – in certain circumstances."

"Exactly," said the Duchess. "And that is why I think we should wait and see how circumstances develop before anything is said about Otto's ancestry. Surprise can be a very effective ally, especially when people are… exhausted. But I would need other allies as well, of course."

"Of course," said Okada. "I am not at this moment able to speak for the Governor-General, since he is still unaware of the situation, but I believe he would think it in the Company's best interests that peace should be restored in North Germany – if it should, unfortunately, be disrupted. And I could envisage a situation in which he would think it appropriate to lend the Company's weight to the… implementation of a compromise solution to a problem which had given rise to conflict.

Needless to say, I shall seek an urgent consultation with him on my return to Antwerp, and I shall advise you of the outcome. Possibly you might think it appropriate for Secretary Steinberg to accompany me, so that he can then return to you with a confidential report on the Governor-General's decision? At this juncture it would seem desirable that as few people as possible should be privy to your thoughts on this delicate subject." He turned towards me and said, with a small gesture of his hand, "And nothing pertaining to our discussion should be recorded in writing."

"As always, I value your wise counsel," said the Duchess, smiling. "Steinberg will be happy to pay a visit to Antwerp, I'm sure. And while he's there he can arrange for the purchase of muskets for a second battalion of Lifeguards that I'm planning to recruit. With troublesome times ahead I can't rely on the levies mobilizing quickly enough when they're needed – besides which, they haven't been trained in your Eastern methods of warfare that everyone wants to copy nowadays."

"Everyone?" Okada queried.

"Frederick and Joseph have both had Honanese officers drilling their household troops for several months now. Didn't you know? It may prove to be something of an embarrassment should they fall out over Brunswick."

"Several months?" said Okada. "I'm afraid my sources have not been so reliable as I expect them to be. I shall have to… make some enquiries. Meanwhile, I'm sure we shall be able to supply enough muskets to meet your immediate needs, at the usual price."

"Well, that's enough about business," said the Duchess briskly. "You know that you're both invited to supper this evening. I'm afraid it's one of those occasions to which a great many people expect to be invited, and so there will not be any opportunity for serious conversation. But we shall do our best to entertain you in our German fashion. Young man," she looked straight into my eyes, "I look forward to seeing how well you can dance."

My instant panic at the thought of having to perform in public must have shown on my face, for she laughed and said, "Don't be alarmed. I can't expect you to be familiar with our quaint old customs. I shall personally teach you the steps."

Smiling, Okada interjected, "Your Grace does us great honour."

“I would offer the same instruction to you,” she said, “but I know that the Company’s High Representative must at all times maintain his dignity, whereas this young man is still – I hope - permitted to put the occasional foot wrong without compromising his employers.”

We made our formal farewells and the secretary conducted us to the door of the tower where we were lodged, making grave conversation with Okada about his pleasure at the prospect of visiting Antwerp and seeing the Company’s development of the city, about which he had heard so much. My mind was full of mixed emotions: excitement at the prospect of seeing the natives in celebratory mood, and trepidation at the thought of being unable to measure up to whatever Terpsichorean test the Duchess might have in store for me.

CHAPTER 3

The banquet was held in the same great hall where we had been received by the Duchess in the morning. A top table for the ruler and some twenty of her most eminent guests occupied the position where her throne had been located, and Okada was seated at her right hand. The other tables were placed at right angles to it, in three long, parallel lines, seating around a hundred of what I assumed to be the cream of Hamburg society. To honour the occasion they had dressed themselves in their most expensive apparel and the result, to my Eastern eyes, was an outlandish medley of colours, materials and ornamentation, with the men more richly attired and accoutred than their wives and daughters. (I assumed that the very few young women present must be daughters of notable guests.)

I found myself seated next to one of these young women at the bottom of one of the lowest tables and, since the middle-aged woman on my other side spoke no Latin, it was to her that all my conversation was addressed. She must have been deliberately selected to be my mentor at dinner, for she immediately made herself known to me, and seemed ready to respond to all my questions, and to question me, intelligently, about Japan and the Company. Her name was Frederika and she was daughter to Count Dietrich von Oldenburgh, who, with his wife, was settled near to the Duchess on the top table. Her hair, like her father's beard, was as yellow as straw, and her eyes were deep blue and seemed to sparkle when anything I said aroused her interest.

Frederika kept me informed about the ingredients in the succession of dishes put before us, some of which were entirely alien to my palate. With her help I also gradually compiled in my mind a list of the notables seated around me. They were mainly high officials of state or aristocrats visiting the ducal court, together with four religious dignitaries who would have upset the gender balance around the tables had it not been for the four daughters who had been invited to accompany their parents. The Duchess, I learnt, like to have some younger women at her court and would often talk informally to them.

While we were eating a group of musicians played in a small gallery to the left of the top table. At first I was almost unaware of them because there was so much else to observe and discover, but towards the end of the meal their playing penetrated to my ear through the incessant clamour of conversation. Music had never been one of my interests and I was only vaguely aware of the changing tunes emanating from the small group of colourfully-clothed minstrels. Then one of them began to play by himself on what, from where I was sitting, looked like a square box that he struck with his fingers, producing a range of tinkling notes that blended together in a remarkable way. As he played the conversations gradually began to subside until everyone was listening. It was unlike any music I had heard before, and when the young man finished his piece people clapped their hands or banged on the tables in applause.

"What instrument was he playing?" I asked; and Frederika replied, "It's called a spinet. It's quite a new invention. I think it came from the south just a few years ago. I've only once before heard one played, when a minstrel troupe from Milan was here last year."

"Where do the minstrels come from?" I asked.

"Like all minstrels, they travel around a lot, but I think they started in Austria. They're known as the Mozart Minstrels, because that's the name of the older man who leads them – the one who was playing the six-stringed instrument. It's called a viola da braccio. The younger man who played the spinet is his son, Amadeus. He composes most of their music, and because he's so good they've become quite famous in all the German Duchies. That's why I know about them. If you want them to come you have to pay them twice as much as any other minstrel troupe. Look! The girl in blue is going to sing and accompany herself on the psaltery. Her name is Aloysia. The other older man is her father, Fridolin Weber."

A sweet-faced girl who can't have been much older than sixteen began to sing in German, accompanying herself by plucking the strings of a triangular-shaped instrument. Its sound reminded me of the East Asian pipa, and for a moment my thoughts were back in the classroom at my old school, where our teacher of Mandarin was reading us a poem from the ancient empire of the T'ang. The poet compared the sound of the pipa to 'pearls falling into a jade plate'. I suppose the quotation was firmly fixed in my mind because, a few months later, it enabled me to answer an examination question.

The song was warmly applauded by the diners, and I noticed that the young minstrel called Amadeus looked at the singer with undisguised admiration. Conversation around the tables then resumed, and the minstrels disappeared from the gallery. “They’ll be getting something to eat,” said Frederika, “before they come down and play for the dancing.”

Her words reminded me of the Duchess’s promise – or threat – and I became apprehensive at the thought of having to display my ineptitude on the dance floor. But then it occurred to me that the beautiful Frederika might be assigned to be my partner, and the possibility that I might be allowed to hold her soft little hand in the course of some cavorting immediately revived my spirits.

“Does everyone take part in the dancing?” I asked.

“No. It’s mostly the younger people. But the Duchess herself is very sprightly, as you’ll see.”

A few minutes later the Duchess rose from her seat and everyone else followed suit. The tables were abandoned and we all moved to the other half of the great hall, where a small door opened to admit the minstrels. They took up their places on a low dais that had been set up against the end wall, and soon began to play.

The first dance was a very formal affair. The Duchess made a gesture with her hand and some twenty people – husbands and wives, I presumed – formed a circle around her, standing at arm’s length from one another. They all seemed to know exactly what was expected of them. While they clapped rhythmically to the music she glided towards Count von Oldenburg and, with much bowing and curtseying, led him back to the centre of the circle. There was then a change in the tempo of the music and, with half the circle moving clockwise and the other half anti-clockwise, it became transformed into an avenue with a canopy of extended arms, down which the Duchess and the Count danced a little jig, hand in hand. Reaching the end they separated and led the two files in opposite directions, until once again the circle was formed, with the Count standing on his own in the centre.

The procedure was repeated again and again and again, until every one of the participants had had a turn at standing in the centre. To me it had the appearance of a totally pointless exercise, only a little less boring for the participants than for the spectators. I assumed that it must have its origins in some ancient tribal ritual, possibly long forgotten.

The second dance was livelier, with couples spending part of the time facing one another, holding hands, and jigging backwards and forwards to a jolly tune. In this dance the younger guests predominated, while their seniors stood around talking in small groups, to which liveried footmen carried trays laden with drinks. When the music ended the dancers had recourse, with much chattering, to their drinks trays.

Suddenly I was aware that the Duchess was standing beside me. "I hope you observed that last dance carefully," she said. "We're going to have it again, and you are going to dance with me."

A sensation of panic spread over me like a heat rash. I was being ordered to make a fool of myself in public. "I… I'm not sure that I completely understood all the steps, Your Grace," I stammered. "Some of the movements were very quick."

"Don't be alarmed," she said, looking directly into my eyes. "I will tell you what to do, and it's said that I am a very good teacher. Just try not to step on my feet."

I bowed in token of my consent, and she took me by the hand and led me towards the musicians' dais. There she halted and made an announcement in her guttural language, presumably saying what the dance was to be. I caught a glimpse of Okada's face, which displayed a mixture of surprise and amusement. And then the musicians began to play – a different tune from the previous one, but with the same kind of lively rhythm. Clumsily I began to move, listening intently for the Duchess's instructions.

She was, indeed, a good teacher, and although my feet did not always go where I intended to put them, I managed to avoid any major blunders. In Japan I am accounted moderately tall, but the northern Europeans are a larger race and, as I had already observed, the Duchess was above the average height for their women. So when the steps of the dance brought us face to face her eyes were on a level with my own. (I later discovered that the heels of her shoes added a little to her height.) Every time that happened she looked intently into my eyes, as though she was searching for something. I was totally unused to being scrutinized by a woman, but found the experience not unpleasant. This powerful woman clearly found me interesting, and I assumed it was because she didn't often find herself in close proximity to someone from Japan. So I tried to return her gaze with a look that showed friendly, but not disrespectful, acceptance of her curiosity. I was sure that that was what Okada would have wanted me to do.

When the music stopped I made a deep bow to the Duchess, and she said, "You learn quickly, young man. If you are going to live in Europa it is good that you should get to know our customs. Frederika," she called out to the young woman, who was standing not far away from us, "our Japanese guest will take the next dance with you. He is a ready learner. Show him the steps."

So I stumbled my way through the next lively dance, which included forming in circles of twelve and gyrating, hand in hand, with a quickening of the tempo each time this exercise was performed. The participants were all out of breath by the end of the final measure. My pretty partner's cheeks were flushed and her eyes were bright with excitement as I made my final bow to her. She was about to say something when the Duchess stepped between us.

"You danced that with great agility," she said, "and you managed to keep off the young lady's toes. But now it is time to allow these people to go home. Follow me," she commanded, and led me through the throng to where Okada was standing, close to the musicians. She spoke briefly to the elder Mozart, no doubt informing him that the party was over, and then turned to Okada.

"I trust that you have enjoyed our little entertainment, simple though it must seem to you," she said, and Okada expressed his gratitude for a delightful evening and the opportunity to observe such pleasant and relaxing customs. "I should like to retain the company of your young companion for a little longer," the Duchess went on. "There's an ancient manuscript in the Latin tongue that I've been trying to decipher, and I'm sure his educated eyes will be able to solve one or two problems for me. I promise I'll return him safely to his quarters when we've looked at it together."

Okada bowed, and with a glance at me which was not seeking approval – as he had no need to – but giving reassurance, replied, "I am sure he will use his best endeavours to be of service to you, Your Grace. I shall have no further need of his assistance tonight, since your generous hospitality has prepared me for immediate retirement to my bed." And he bowed again.

So, when the formalities of bringing the evening to a close had been completed and the guests had departed, the Duchess led me once again to the room where we had had our meeting that morning. This time we were alone.

The Duchess went immediately to some bookshelves which I hadn't noticed on my previous visit; nor had my eyes taken in the large tapestry hanging on the wall to which my back had been turned when I was sitting at the table. It was rather clumsily executed, but clearly depicted a naked woman with long yellow hair being presented with an apple by a kneeling man, accompanied by a large dog. Underneath the tapestry there was what I took to be a armless couch covered with a rug woven in a brightly coloured pattern. Altogether, the room was less like a venue for official business than I had remembered it.

"This is the book," she said, carefully lifting a very decrepit-looking volume from one of the shelves and placing it gently on the table. When she opened it I could see that the pages were hand written, and I remembered reading in Arima's *History and Religions of Europa* that a Taiwanese who set up a printing press in Genoa had been impaled on its screw by order of the Sultan – a painful punctuation which had discouraged any imitators. And when the Empire began to disintegrate the Christian priests, according to Arima, had persuaded their new rulers to perpetuate the ban on printing, because the existence of cheap books would encourage the common people to learn to read, and this would make them insubordinate to God and their superiors. However, the volume on the table looked as if it long predated the invention of printing.

I leaned forward to examine the open pages and was relieved to discover that the letters were recognizable as those that I had been taught. "If it's very old I may not be able to understand all the words," I said. "I learned only the Latin that you speak today. We were told about the writings of ancient times, but we didn't study them"

"I think you'll recognize most of the words," she said. "The book was written about sixteen hundred years ago, when there was still a Roman Empire. But this copy was made only about five hundred years ago, not long before the Mongols came. The author was a man called Lucius Apuleius, who was a pagan – not a Christian, you understand. That's why I've not asked any of my own Latin experts to help me with it. They're all priests, and they wouldn't approve of it – though there are one or two of them who would probably like to take it away to read behind closed doors." She laughed, a deep, chuckling laugh.

"Now take a look at this passage," she continued, carefully turning over several pages, "and tell me what you make of it."

I scrutinized the writing and discovered I had little difficulty in making sense of it. If the Duchess was fluent in Latin, which she appeared to be, I couldn't understand why she had had a problem with it.

"Can you read it out to me?" she asked.

"I shall do my best, Your Grace," I replied. My eyes went back to the top of the page and I began to read.

So when I had refreshed myself with wine and was now ready for love, not only in mind but also in body, I took off my clothes and showing Fotis my great impatience I said, 'Oh sweetheart take pity on me and help me, for you see I am now prepared for the battle, which you yourself appointed. After I felt the first arrow of cruel Cupid in my breast I bent my bow strongly and now fear – because it is bent so hard – that my string may break. But so that you may please me better, let down your hair and come and fondly embrace me.' At which she made no delay, but pushed aside the food and wine and undressed herself, and let down her hair, presenting her loving body to me in the manner of beautiful Venus when she goes under the waves of the sea.

'Now," said she, 'the hour of jousting has come. Now has come the time of war. So show yourself like a man, for I will not retreat. I will not fly the field. See that you are valiant, see that you are courageous, for there is no appointed time for our skirmish to end.'

Saying these words she came to me in bed and sweetly embraced me.

I put my hand on the page to turn it but the Duchess said, "That will be enough for now. You read it very well. Tell me, do you have books like that in Japan?"

My mind went back to a Sunga book, ancient in origin but frequently reprinted, which had greatly excited me at about the age of fourteen. "Yes, we do. Some were written a long time ago, like this book, but others are more recent. How does this story go on?"

"The hero is accidentally turned into an ass by the woman Fotis, and has a lot of painful adventures before he prays to the Egyptian goddess, Isis, who turns him back into a man. It's a silly story but some of the episodes in it are very amusing, like the one you've just been reading. Tell me, have you yet had the good fortune to meet with a woman like Fotis?"

She was looking at me very intently with her large, blue eyes, and I noticed that her cheeks were flushed. At that moment I began to realize that I might not have been brought to her private room because of my skills as a translator. She was a widow and, by Okada's account, had not so long ago lost her most recent lover. Was it possible that what she really wanted was for me to make love to her? She was an absolute ruler, albeit of a petty principality, and I was the lowliest of junior employees, although in a company that was a powerful force in this part of the world. Maybe it was novelty that attracted her – the fact that I was Japanese. I couldn't believe it was any other aspect of my physical appearance, for I had never thought of myself as handsome.

Those were the thoughts that flashed through my mind as I stammered my reply. "No… no, Your Grace, I… I've not yet had that good fortune." This was true, though many of my contemporaries would have found it difficult to believe. But I was among the small, if increasing, minority of young men in East Asia who held to the belief that, in the new Age of Rational Behaviour, to have sex in the absence of mutual desire was demeaning to the man as well as to the woman. It was a viewpoint derided by traditionalists but that made it all the more attractive to modern-minded young people. So, although temptation had often been strong and my purse had seldom been empty, I was still a virgin. Of course, my father had taken me to his favourite geisha when I was sixteen; but geishas are not prostitutes, and that encounter had been educational rather than physical.

"Really?" exclaimed the Duchess. "How very interesting. Is that because you don't… find women desirable, or perhaps because you don't want to do it with a woman below your station and others have not been… available?" She looked at me quizzically as I struggled to find the most appropriate answer.

I was thinking in Japanese and it took more effort than usual to find the Latin words to express my thoughts. "I find women very desirable, Your Grace," I replied, "but I have wanted to… to be with a woman who also found me desirable – for myself and not for money – and so far I have not met such a woman."

She smiled, revealing white, even teeth, and I sensed that my reply had met with her approval. "And if you were to meet such a woman – one who longed to hold your strong young body in her arms and feel the vigour of your passionate embrace – would you want to give her pleasure?"

"I would, indeed, Your Grace," I replied; and then realizing that I hadn't yet felt that stirring in my loins which only a short time before had surprised me when Frederika's soft hand touched my own during the dance, I added, "But, of course, I would have much to learn, and on the first occasion might not give as much pleasure as I would want to give."

"Your humility is commendable," she said, stretching out her hand and patting my shoulder. "Many a poor girl has been bitterly disappointed by a brash young fellow whose only aim was to prove to himself that he was able to scatter his seed. What you need for your first encounter is an experienced woman who can show you what to do if your aim is to give pleasure as well as to receive it. Would you not agree?"

"That would, indeed, be a perfect way to begin, Your Grace."

"Then is it not fortunate, for me as well as for you, that tonight I have a little time to spare which I can spend on your instruction?" she asked, moving closer to me, so that I could smell the musky perfume she was wearing – almost certainly an Eastern scent, for I was sure I had encountered it somewhere before. As her blue eyes looked interrogatively into mine she again stretched out her hand, and this time gently stroked the side of my head, her soft fingertips coming to rest on my neck.

For a moment a conflict of contradictory emotions seemed to paralyze my limbs. To have my first erotic encounter with this splendid, and apparently understanding, woman could be an ideal introduction to the mysteries of sex. But even though her proximity was beginning to excite me I had not yet felt the physical urge that I knew was going to be needed if I was to perform the act of intercourse. Although her face was attractive, in a Western fashion, I needed something more to arouse my lust.

It was as though she read my thoughts for she said, very softly, "But you don't yet know what a Western woman looks like, do you? Perhaps we are different from the women of your homeland. I've never seen a Japanese woman. But you can judge for yourself, and then we shall discover whether your passions can be excited by what Europa has to offer."

With that she began to unfasten the silver clasps that held her elaborately embroidered gown in place. I watched in astonishment as she pulled it down off her shoulders, gleaming white in the soft light from the six candles in the chandelier above our heads. With a wriggle of her hips she freed it from her body, and it fell in a heap on the floor. Taking a step backward, she kicked off her pointed, red leather shoes. Her undergarment was a white linen shirt with lace-trimmed cuffs and collar that reached to just below her knees, and her legs were encased in white stockings of some fine material.

I felt my heart begin to beat more rapidly in anticipation of what I knew must be about to follow. With a swift movement of her crossed arms she drew the shirt up, over her head, and tossed it to one side. Apart from her stockings, each secured in mid-thigh by a dark blue garter, she stood before me naked in the candlelight.

Instinctively I knelt down on one knee in token of respect for what had been revealed to me. Although her hips and thighs were heavy her waist was still narrow, and her breasts looked firm (not that I had ever seen anything with which to compare them, apart from a few pictures). "I… I've never seen anything so beautiful," I stammered.

"I'm sure there are more beautiful bodies that you could discover," she said, with a hint of a smile on her lips, "But this is the one you're able to see, and I'm glad that you find it beautiful. Now it's time to have a look at you. I will help you to reveal yourself." I remembered with a sense of relief that I had put on clean underwear to attend the dinner.

She beckoned to me to get up and approach her. Then, with muttered impatience at the unfamiliar Eastern-style fastenings on my tunic, she began to undress me. The nearness of her naked body and the eagerness with which she was tugging at my clothing set my heart racing even faster, so that I was sure she must be able to hear it pounding in my chest. And I instantly had no doubt that I would be able to perform whatever she might want from me.

I was not mistaken. Like Apuleius in the story I found it hard to contain my eagerness, but the Duchess kept me firmly under her instruction. From inside a little case that had been made to look like a book on the shelf she produced a small narrow pouch made of some soft, slippery material. Saying, "My physician tells me I am not yet entirely past the time when there is still a risk of nine-month consequences," she slipped it on and fastened it at the base with a little drawstring.

"Do you have these clever devices in Japan?" she asked, taking my hand and leading me to the couch.

"I have heard of them, but never before have I seen one," I replied, feeling glad that the device was not diminishing my enthusiasm.

"It is fortunate they are not easier to come by," she commented. "If every peasant's wife could lay her hands on a supply of them it would not be long before we would be running short of hands to do the work – and to fight the wars."

She stretched herself out on the couch, leaving room for me to lie down beside her. Was she now expecting me to take command of the situation, I wondered, as the touch of her soft warm flesh against my arm and thigh made me gasp with excitement.

"Contain yourself a little longer," she said, "and I will show you how to make me – or any warm-blooded woman – as eager for the act of love as you already are." And she did.

In my inexperience, mitigated only be reading a few pillow books and hearing the bawdy reminiscences of fellow-students, I had formed the vague impression that women's pleasure in lovemaking was derived mainly from their satisfaction at being able to give pleasure to their partners. The Duchess very quickly dispelled that illusion. Within minutes she was guiding my fingers, my lips and my tongue so that her body seemed to have become a complex musical implement, emitting sighs and gasps and groans in response to my caresses.

My own excitement was mounting to a frenzy when she suddenly exclaimed, "I must not be cruel. It's your first time and you need to shoot your bolt. It won't take you long, and then we can start again." Her strong thighs took hold of my body in a firm embrace and I needed no more guidance.

As she had predicted, it was all over in less than a dozen thrusts and I lay panting in her arms. But she seemed well pleased with my efforts, kissing my damp forehead and saying, "You have a good blend of tenderness and passion. Is that just you, I wonder, or is it a characteristic of your race?"

I didn't need long to refuel my desire, and soon the kissing and caressing had begun again – but not before the Duchess had supplied me with fresh protection against any consequences of our passion. As we embraced again my confidence increased and I turned her over to explore with lips and fingertips the delightful landscape of her back. She then introduced me to the excitement of an alternative position in which to consummate our passion. And this time I was able so to control my eagerness that I could move from one position to another and keep her in what appeared to be an ecstasy of enjoyment for more than half-an-hour.

Afterwards, as we lay side by side on our backs, our bodies touching lightly at shoulder and hip, the Duchess said, "You are an apt pupil. I hope you will make good use of what I have taught you. Remember that whatever woman you take to your bed, whether she be a peasant girl or a great lady, if your first thought is to give her pleasure then you'll be well rewarded in the pleasure that you receive from her."

"You have convinced me of that, Your Grace," I replied.

"When we're alone together you must call me Sophy," she said, "but only when we're alone. This pleasure that we have had must always be something private that casts no shadow when we walk in public. I'm sure you understand that."

"Yes, I do, Your… Sophy."

"You're probably thinking about what you ought to tell your master, Okada," she went on. "You may tell him what has happened between us, for he is certain to guess it; and he will understand, I think, and will not be angry with you. Of course, he will hope that you have learned some useful secrets from me. That is his occupation. And he will hope that you have not given away any secrets to me." She laughed, a deep, throaty chuckle.

"I don't think I know any secrets to give away. I've only just arrived in Europa," I said, relieved that I was not being asked to lie to Okada about what had happened.

"You might be surprised at what qualifies as a secret," she said. "We all have our spies, but often they are so busy counting the numbers of big guns in a fortress or watching which important people are visiting each other that they miss the really important details. For example, do you know the real reason why Okada came to see me?"

"Wasn't it to sign the agreement about selling fish?"

"That was important, but we'd already agreed the details by exchanging letters. He could have sent it with somebody who is not as busy as he is. And when he left Antwerp he didn't know about old Brunswick being on his death-bed – or did he?"

"No, I'm sure he didn't."

"Exactly. That's just the kind of secret that you can tell me, and nobody else could."

"But do you think the Company is your enemy, so that you need to have spies to watch us?" I asked, emboldened by her frankness.

"In the business of statecraft it is better not to think in terms of 'enemies' and 'friends'. Something could happen that would make today's ally tomorrow's adversary. It is best to keep a watch on everyone. But I hope the Company will go on being my ally for many years to come."

She raised herself on one elbow and looked down at me. "You are a clever young man and I'm sure you will rise quickly in the service of the Company. I would be interested to hear what you think about Europa as you go around with Okada and see things with fresh eyes. Will you write to me sometimes – I'll tell you how to send the letters? This is not for statecraft. It would be personal, for the things we could learn from each other. Tonight I've taught you a little bit about women, but I know quite a lot about men, too, and that could be useful to you."

"I would like to correspond with you," I said, surprised by her offer. "But you won't expect me to tell you any secrets, will you?"

"No, of course not. What I want to understand is the way that you East Asians think, and what is different in the way that you do things from the way that we have always done them here in Europa. I believe we've got to learn new ways to do things if we're ever going to be rich and powerful again, like they say we were before the Mongols and the Turks came and destroyed the old kingdoms of Christendom."

She was sitting fully upright now, looking down at me with eyes that sparkled with a different kind of passion. "It's only about thirty years since we started breaking free from the Sultan and his Pashas, and that wouldn't have happened if the Magyars hadn't smashed his army. Leaders like my late husband's grandfather seized their chance; but once they were free they just continued to do things in the way that the Pashas had been doing them. The fighting men and the priests were happy – most of the time – to let them give the orders, and share out the plunder. But I don't think the peasants have seen very much change. And now that we've stopped fighting the Sultan we're divided against each other, so that if someone else came along – maybe one of the Pashas after he'd swallowed up a few of the other pashaliks to make himself powerful, or the Slav Emperor if he stopped fighting the Ottomans – we'd be too weak to resist and once again our little states would disappear."

"How do you think that could be prevented?" I asked.

"We have to learn new ways of doing things," she said vehemently. "It's no use looking back to the past. Joseph of Austria would like to revive the old Holy Roman Empire – with himself as Emperor, of course – but that's not going to happen. Frederick of Brandenburg, I suspect, would like to gobble up his neighbours and make himself a kingdom that would have more men and more money. That's a more practical idea, but he's getting to be too old now, and his *Junkers* won't let him change his army in the way his Honanese adviser tells him he ought to – or so I've heard."

"Have the Honanese really got someone in Brandenburg?" I exclaimed, raising myself on one elbow when I heard this disturbing news.

The Duchess smiled at my reaction. "It will not be long before you are as clever a dealer in secrets as your master," she said. "But I think you'll find that Okada already knows about it. What I would like to understand is how you East Asians have become so strong that you can send your ships around the world to buy and sell, and your merchants have become so rich that they can have their own armies. Why was the Pasha of the Netherlands defeated at Passchendaele when he had more guns and far more soldiers than your Company could bring against him? And the same thing happened again, seven years later, when the Sultan and the Pasha of Lorraine moved against the Company and you scattered their combined armies at Briey. There is no shortage of bold warriors in Europa, and nowadays there are plenty of guns as well, but you Asians have a different way of doing things and it must be because you think in a different way. If we're going to have a new, strong Christendom in this continent we need to be able to think like you do.

"That's why I'd like you to write to me. But I'd also like you to come back soon, if Okada will let you, so we can do again what we've just been doing. With you there are no complications like there would be if I took a young man from Holstein – and you're a lusty young fellow, as I knew you would be the moment I saw you walk into my hall."

She bent her head and gave me a lingering kiss on my lips that instantly rekindled my desire. But when I stretched out my hand to cup her breast she removed it, laughing, and told me it was time for me to leave.

CHAPTER 4

The Council Chamber in Antwerp Castle was a stark and forbidding room. On my first visit to it the gloom was lightened by shafts of Spring sunlight through the two tall, narrow windows in its east wall, one on either side of the much-needed blue-tiled stove. The centre of the room was occupied by a table some six metres long and a metre and a half wide. On the south side sat the four government-appointed members of the West Europa Company Regulatory Council and facing them were the Governor-General and four Senior Factors, including my boss, Okada. At one end of the table sat Vice-Admiral Katsura, commander of the West Europa Squadron of the Imperial Navy, and at the other end was General Kuroki, commander-in-chief of all the troops, Imperial and Company, in West Europa.

I was overawed to be in the presence of so many powerful men. My reason for being there was to fetch and carry papers for Okada, and I was positioned along with five other secretaries at three small tables placed along the north wall of the room, behind the backs of our bosses. I shared my table with Miyamoto, secretary to Senior Factor and Grand Treasurer Yamaguchi. He was a morose young man whom I had met for the first time that morning.

Governor-General Higashi opened the proceedings with a few formal remarks, and the Minutes were read out by his secretary, Masaki, who was positioned at the table next to mine. Higashi had been described to me by Okada as "a man in a desperate hurry – he wants to consolidate the Company's position before the Augsburg Sultan's power completely disintegrates." Before the meeting began he had acknowledged my introductory bow with a warm smile that transformed his austere and anxious-looking face. I was eager to see how he would relate to the four Councillors, appointed by the government in Edo to 'advise' him. Everyone knew that their real job was to warn him if Company policy seemed to be coming into conflict with national interest – as conceived of by the government, which five years earlier had lent the Company a million yen when its revenue had plunged after the great plague and famine in the Netherlands.

"When we last met we were much exercised by the reports of banditry and extortion in the districts of Liege and Namur, and the police corruption that appeared to be protecting the bandits," said

Higashi crisply, when the Minutes had been agreed. “You will recall that I decided to replace our somewhat elderly Collector with young Nodzu, and give him a company of the Walloon Native Infantry and a squadron of the Flanders Guides to assist his efforts. I am pleased to tell you that already he has made significant progress. Two marauding bands of ruffians have been intercepted and destroyed before they could escape back to their lairs in the Ardennes Forest. Nodzu informs me that he has displayed their heads at strategic crossing–points on the frontier with the Pashalik of Lorraine, so that any others who may have bolted across to there will receive the message. And with the threat of reprisals lifted some village elders have already been willing to come forward and identify rogue elements in the district police troop.”

“That sounds very encouraging,” said a short, swarthy Councillor, whose name, Yamaguchi’s secretary informed me in a whisper, was Baron Nagata. “But the absence of any effective law enforcement in Lorraine must remain a source of anxiety. From what I hear the Pasha himself is the biggest bandit of the lot, though fortunately his depredations have so far been confined to his own subjects.”

“Very true,” replied Higashi, “but I have informed Major Sugino, who is in command of the troops supporting the civil power, that he shouldn’t hesitate to exercise the right of hot pursuit if his men encounter any of the ruffians making a run for the border – the precise whereabouts of which are, anyhow, unknown.”

“But surely this would not be a good moment to provoke an incident with the Pasha?” asked the Councillor sitting to the right of Nagata. (His name, I Iearned later, was Hiraoka.)

“I don’t think we need worry about that,” Higashi replied. “Pasha Yussuf still owes us the hundred thousand dinars he borrowed two years ago to pay his army, when the Sultan and the Pasha of Franconia were threatening him. And from what I hear, now that the money has all gone he’s having to let some of his war bands depart. The Swiss have already gone home to their mountains.”

“I’d be surprised if they departed empty-handed,” said Baron Nagata. “They’ll have left a few empty barns and cowsheds along their route.”

“There is one other item related to law and order which, you may recall, Lord Justice Oku raised at our last meeting,” said Higashi. “Unfortunately he can’t be here today because he’s suffering from a fever. It’s the question of whether we ought to act to suppress the superstitious practice that the natives have of burning alive people – usually elderly women – whom they believe to be ‘witches’. There have recently been several incidents in Holland and Brabant, and the Collectors were uncertain how they ought to react. As I see it, the question is straightforward. Do I issue a decree banning this barbaric practice, or do we turn a blind eye to it?”

“Well, you know my views, Excellency,” said Hiraoka. “The Company is here to do business, and to keep the peace so that business can be done. It should not be interfering with the customs of the natives in ways that might provoke their hostility and so disturb the peace. Of course this custom is cruel and barbaric, but it’s not so long since very similar beliefs were widely accepted in Japan, and I’m sure among the peasantry they still prevail, even today. Wherever there is a primitive religion you find cruelty, but there is little that outsiders can do to change it.”

Hiraoka leaned forward in his seat and looked to his left along the table, as though challenging his colleagues to disagree.

The Councillor on Nagata’s left took up the challenge. By a process of elimination I identified him as Count Furaya, whose reputation as the leading authority on the antiquities of Europa was well established. Lean-faced and grey-haired, he had a somewhat ascetic appearance, and his voice was quiet and relaxed.

“I would concur with Councillor Hiraoka’s opinion that changing ancient superstitions is a difficult and challenging task, Your Excellency,” he said. “But it is surely not impossible when you consider the changes that have taken place in our country over the past hundred years. We have seen how the discoveries of the natural sciences and the application of rational thinking have transformed ancient institutions and liberated at least the educated classes from groundless fears and superstitious practices. Ought we not to share these benefits with people for whose direction we have assumed responsibility, so that we may earn their gratitude and hope, one day, to win their full co-operation in the management of the commonwealth? I recognize that initially we shall encounter hostility from fanatical believers in this particular superstitious practice; but it isn't something central to the religious beliefs of the Christians.

"I have talked to one of their leaders, the Bishop of Antwerp, and he seemed almost embarrassed when I raised the question of witchcraft. What he was much more concerned about was protecting the property of the various religious institutions. As you are no doubt aware, the Christians have monasteries, just as we have in Asia, and these, together with their temples – which they call 'churches' – are endowed with land and money by the believers. Under the Pashas they were constantly being robbed, and so the Bishop is extremely nervous about what the Company's attitude might be.

"This encourages me to think that we might be able to enlist the support of the religious leaders for abolishing the offensive practice of witch-burning. Might I make a suggestion, Your Excellency?"

"By all means, Count Furaya," said Higashi. "I think I perceive the direction in which your thoughts are leading you."

"My suggestion is that Your Excellency might consult discreetly with the key religious leaders in the province. They could be advised that if they were willing to give their unequivocal support to a decree outlawing the practice of witch-burning and any other persecution of alleged witches it would be accompanied by another decree guaranteeing the property of religious institutions – which should also include the mosques of the Muslims and the synagogues of the Jews – against any confiscation or taxation. I would be surprised if they didn't accept the bargain."

Higashi nodded his head three times, very deliberately. "That sounds to me like a prudent and practical suggestion," he said. "If successful it could do a great deal to secure the peace, and not just on this issue of witchcraft. Superstitious people seem very willing to submit to those whom they believe to be in communication with supernatural powers. That can be of considerable value in the maintenance of law and order. One priest can be as useful as a hundred policemen – and a lot cheaper to maintain."

"On the other hand, Your Excellency," said Hiraoka, "the reverse can be equally true. If the priests are at variance with government they can stir up the superstitious rabble in ways that can be exceedingly expensive."

“All the more reason, Councillor Hiraoka, why we should take this opportunity to tie the religious hierarchy into an agreement that will make them dependent on our goodwill,” said Higashi. “Does anyone think that I ought not to pursue Count Furaya’s proposition?”

There was a general murmur of assent around the table and Higashi gave three quick nods of his head before proceeding to the next business, which was my master, Okada’s report on the successful conclusion of the fish supply agreement with the Duchess of Holstein.

For the first time in the meeting the fourth Council member, Akiyama, had something to say. “This is a promising development, Your Excellency,” he said when Okada had finished speaking, “but we should see it as merely the beginning of something which has huge commercial potential. As you may be aware, the Dutch fishermen from whom the Company obtains its supplies, range as far across the Northern Sea as their small craft will allow them to sail. But if we are to increase demand to the maximum – and virtually the whole of the sub-continent is a potential market – it will very quickly outstrip supply. Now I have heard that the Shantungese Company has begun building larger vessels for some of the British fishermen whom they use, so that they can travel to fishing grounds in the northern part of what they call the Atlantic Ocean. The resources over there are said to be limitless. If we are to obtain a commanding position in this trade we would be well advised to emulate them.”

“I fully agree, Your Excellency,” said Count Furaya. “There is some historical evidence to suggest that the northern European coastlands produced very competent seamen, manning sizeable vessels, in the centuries before the Turkish conquest gave a monopoly of seaborne trade to merchants from Mediterranean ports. We have had no difficulty in reviving ship-building for the Company’s own use in Antwerp and Rotterdam, and in Bordeaux. It would make excellent sense to encourage our local fishermen to expand their range and venture into the ocean – perhaps by giving them loans for the construction of larger vessels.”

In the short discussion that followed there appeared to be general agreement that this policy should be pursued, and the Senior Factor responsible for trade, Matsuzaki, who was sitting at the Governor-General’s right hand, was given responsibility for taking it forward. Concluding the discussion, Higashi remarked, “In your forthcoming visit to Britain, Count Furaya, you may well be able to garner some further information about the competition which appears to be developing there."

He then called on Okada to introduce what he described as, "the most important item on our agenda, the impending dispute about the succession to the Duchy of Brunswick."

"Yesterday we had confirmation," said Okada, "that Duke Maximilian had finally succumbed to his illness, at the age of fifty-seven. He has left no heir apparent, but I understand that a distant cousin called Franz, who lives in the duchy, has staked a claim to the title. Since he happens to be married to a daughter of Frederick, Duke of Brandenburg, he can rely on strong support from his father-in-law. But a first cousin of the late Duke, named Caroline, is married to a nephew of Joseph, Archduke of Austria, and that ambitious gentleman has already backed her claim, and has started canvassing support among the other dukes."

"Is it not an ancient custom in these German dukedoms that succession is solely through the male line?" asked Count Furaya. "I remember reading about something to that effect called the Salic Law."

"What Count Furaya says is, indeed, true, Your Excellency," said Okada, "but both these candidates base their claims on the relationship of their mothers to the founder of the dynasty. And I learnt on my recent visit to Holstein that there is actually a third candidate, hitherto unmentioned, whose claim derives from his grandmother."

"Who is he?" asked Furaya.

"The third possible claimant is Otto, the sixteen-year-old son of the Duchess of Holstein."

"And what do you expect to happen now?" asked Higashi. "Is there going to be a war beyond our north-eastern frontier?"

"I fear that there is, Your Excellency," Okada replied. "Frederick has already begun to move in support of his son-in-law, who is not at all popular with most of the aristocracy in Brunswick. It will take Joseph longer to get moving, and he has farther to go, but I hear he has already negotiated the support of Augustus of Saxony, which has a short frontier with Brunswick. No doubt Augustus will be expecting payment for his support, possibly the south-eastern district of Kassel, or maybe he has his eye on a slice of Brandenburg."

"And what about Sophia of Holstein?" Higashi asked.

"She, Your Excellency, will be keeping her powder dry – to begin with. Count Oldenburg has begun to mobilize her army, but I believe she will refrain from making a move until the other two have fought it out. And then I think she will move against the winner, hoping to find him weakened by losses and exertion. You will be aware that she has just purchased a considerable quantity of arms and ammunition from the Company."

"I hope she's paid for it," said Akiyama.

"In silver bullion," said Okada, allowing himself a smile.

"Your Excellency, is this a conflict in which we ought to be taking an interest?" asked General Kuroki. "The outcome could well have consequences for the Company."

"It is, and we are," Higashi replied. "At my request Okada is ensuring that we have continuing and reliable intelligence on the situation as it develops. And my next request is to you, General. We must have an effective expeditionary force in readiness to intervene should the need – or the opportunity – arise. Would you agree that Enschede would be an appropriate place at which to assemble such a force?"

"Yes, indeed, Your Excellency, assuming that the requirement might be to move rapidly on the cities of Hanover or Brunswick."

"With respect, Your Excellency, you are surely not proposing that the Company should involve itself in this conflict?" asked Councillor Hiraoka in a voice that sounded genuinely alarmed.

"We are involved whether or not we wish to be," Higashi replied. "Any change in the balance of power on our north-eastern frontier will affect the Company's security. We know that Frederick of Brandenburg is taking subsidies from the Honanese, and sooner or later they will be requiring value for their money. Joseph of Austria has grandiose ambitions to unite the German princes, and taking over Brunswick might give him the momentum that he needs. Caroline has so far proved to be a reliable ally, and our latest treaty with her will open up the hinterland along the Ems, the Weser and the Elbe to our fish trade."

"So is it your intention to give her military support against the others?" asked Hiraoka.

"That may not be necessary. What we do not want to see is Holstein being defeated, and perhaps subsequently overrun, by either of the other duchies. But if Caroline is able to win her own battles we may be able to intervene at the end of the conflict as an impartial mediator, seeking to restore the peace. It would be greatly in our interests to have Brunswick conjoined with Holstein to form a solid buffer in the north-east and, should need arise, a potential ally against the Pasha of Lorraine. At the same time we might well be able to avoid alienating either Frederick of Joseph. But if we are to achieve this result we need to have a credible force under arms and able to move swiftly to wherever it might be needed. General, what units could be made available within the next two weeks?"

"I am sure, Your Excellency, that we could muster five battalions of native infantry and two imperial battalions, with seven, or possibly eight squadrons."

"And artillery?" Higashi enquired. "It's important to show them the guns."

"There would be two heavy batteries and three light, and the galloper troop, of course."

"Your Excellency," Hiraoka interjected, "if General Kuroki's force does become involved in the hostilities there can be no certainty of a speedy conclusion. The Company could find itself sucked into a continuing conflict, with no limit to the expense that will be entailed – unless, of course, you're planning to plunder the ducal coffers in Brunswick. Once again I have to reiterate my view that the Company should avoid involving itself in the politics of the sub-continent. It is here to earn money for its shareholders, and if the natives are unwilling to trade peacefully it should find another market, and leave them to get on with the business of slaughtering, pillaging and raping each other, which appears to have been their principal occupation in recent centuries."

No one around the table appeared to be particularly surprised by this outburst, and I guessed that they had heard Councillor Hiraoka express his opinion on more than one occasion. Count Furaya, however, was quick to respond.

"Your Excellency, while I understand the Honourable Councillor's concern for the Company's profitability, I believe that he underestimates both the cost of failing to keep secure what has already been invested in this sub-continent and the possibility of making it a peaceful and progressive place in which to do business, to the great benefit not only of the Company but also of the inhabitants. I admit that it may take a generation or two fully to achieve that end, but already we have made a promising start.

"Councillor Hiraoka speaks of the natives' propensity for violence," he continued, "but I would suggest that this is no more inevitable than were our own civil conflicts in Japan a century ago. From what we know of its history Europa appears to have enjoyed some periods of relative tranquillity. The last was about a hundred and fifty years ago, when the Taiwanese were already trading here. But when Sultan Bayezid died, not long after the Company established its first factory at Bordeaux, his successors were unable to sustain firm control from Augsburg and the gradual disintegration began.

"We shouldn't forget, however, that in years long past, before the arrival of foreign conquerors, these Europeans invented for themselves such things as the horse-drawn plough, the water-mill and the windmill, and built themselves substantial and beautiful temples and castles, some of which are still in use today. And their religion, even though we have just been talking about one of its uglier manifestations, has many admirable features. It preaches compassion for the poor, obedience to the law, respect for women and sober behaviour. I believe these people have the capacity to learn the lessons of East Asia's 'Tsunami of Reason', and to become partners with us in creating a prosperous future for their children.

"But to begin that process we have to establish civil peace, and I agree with Your Excellency that we must give active support to local rulers who show the potential for good government, and where they don't exist sometimes take over that responsibility ourselves. It's a pity we don't have sufficient power to prevent this forthcoming conflict in Brunswick, but it is right that we should use such power as we have to secure an outcome that will increase the Company's security."

"Thank you, Count Furaya," said Higashi. "That is what I intend to do."

"I wish you luck, Your Excellency," said Councillor Akiyama. "For my part, I would encourage the rascals to buy all the guns they can pay for and let them get on with it. We can always pick up the pieces afterwards."

"I am not sure about selling them guns," General Kuroki interjected. "Powder and ball, perhaps, but you can never be certain in which direction guns will eventually be aimed. Even today's ally can sometimes turn out to be tomorrow's enemy."

"Very true, General," Higashi observed. "We need to be more discriminating than the Honanese. They seem willing to arm anyone who promises to damage the Company. And that reminds me of another matter for concern. Edo informs me that they're concerned about signs of some kind of understanding beginning to develop between Honan and Shantung. In the event of any future resumption of hostilities back in Asia we could find ourselves confronted with a threat from Britain – possibly serving as a base for a Honanese squadron."

"We could very quickly make the Shantungese regret that they ever got mixed up in that kind of arrangement," said Vice-Admiral Katsura, "provided, of course, that they didn't get news of hostilities before we did. We can't afford to be taken by surprise."

"Is there any real likelihood of another war?" asked Baron Nogata. "I should have thought that after what happened… fourteen years ago, is it?... the Honanese would have more sense than to try another round with us."

"So one might think, Baron," said Higashi. "But according to the dispatches I received yesterday things have not been going well in the Government's altercation with the colonists in the New Continent, and there is some apprehension that the Honanese, and others, might be tempted to try fishing in troubled waters. We have to be prepared for all eventualities."

"Your Excellency," said Count Furaya, "you may recall that I have arranged to visit Britain next week, in the course of my antiquarian studies. I shall be meeting the Shantungese Deputy Governor, who is a fellow-enthusiast. I wonder if this might provide an opportunity for some discreet reconnaissance, should the Admiral wish to send a suitably qualified person along with me. As it happens, my secretary is only just recovering from a fever, and it would be better that he did not accompany me. So that role could be occupied by one of the Admiral's officers."

“Sounds like an excellent idea,” said Vice-Admiral Katsura. “There’s a lieutenant on my staff who has sharp eyes and a good head on his shoulders. But will you need to have someone who speaks Latin if you’re having dealings with the natives? Trouble is nobody speaks their language. What’s it called? – English?”

“Yes, it might be a disadvantage not having a Latin speaker with me,” said Furaya.

“That problem could be solved,” interjected my boss, Okada. “If Count Furaya is willing to add a junior secretary to his entourage I would be willing to let him borrow young Hashimoto for a couple of weeks. He’s a fluent speaker of Latin and proved his mettle on our recent trip to Holstein.”

And so it was decided that I should accompany Count Furaya on his visit to Britain.

CHAPTER 5

The brig in which we had sailed from Antwerp dropped anchor in the Pool of London. It was evident from the number of vessels, large and small, that we had passed on our way up river just how busy this centre of the Shantungese West Europa Company's activities had become. Substantial warehouses lined the wharves, and a multitude of ferries, lighters and smaller boats of every kind had traversed the waters of the estuary during the last few miles of our voyage.

Soon after we dropped anchor the ship's longboat was brought alongside to convey Count Furaya, Lieutenant Hirose and myself ashore. We were rowed a short distance upstream towards a huge fortress that dominated the many buildings clustered around it. Pointing towards the looming walls, Furaya said, "That's the famous Tower of London. It was begun about seven hundred years ago. The tall, square tower with the four turrets is the oldest part. When the Taiwanese took over they strengthened the outer fortifications, and mounted guns, of course. And now the Shantungese Company use it as their headquarters."

A brisk squall of rain struck us, and we kept our heads down until we came alongside some stone steps leading up from the river to a fortified gateway in an outer wall of the Tower. As we stepped ashore a native corporal in the dark blue uniform of the Shantungese Company's troops hurried down to meet us. The Count showed him a letter he'd received from the Deputy Governor and this appeared to satisfy him. We were ushered through the gate, past a bored-looking sentry with yellow hair and a very pale skin. In the guardroom we waited until a young Shantungese lieutenant came hurrying to greet us.

He conducted us across a narrow open space to another fortified gateway set in the high inner wall of the fortress. Pointing upward as we entered, he said in halting Latin, "The natives call this building the Bloody Tower. It seems that , hundreds of years ago, one of their kings murdered his deceased brother's children, who were housed in it at the time." We emerged into a wide open space surrounding the massive central keep (which I learned later was called the White Tower – though it was, in fact a dirty grey in colour, stained, no doubt by the smoke of the city's innumerable chimneys).

It was in the White Tower that Deputy Governor Wang Yen-wu had his office. He welcomed us effusively, using the Latin language, in which he appeared to share Count Furaya's fluency. Their exchange brought a look of bewilderment to the face of Lieutenant Hirose, who knew very little Latin. The Count introduced him as "a trusted supercargo of the Company" who was going to advise on the safe transportation back to Antwerp of any artistic purchases that he might make in Britain. After a few more polite exchanges we were invited to sit down at a square, oaken table and a British servant brought us tea.

"I hope that before long you may be able to visit Antwerp and see my collection," said the Count. "There are several pieces of religious art that I acquired in Naples on which I would greatly value your opinion."

"I should be fascinated to see them," the Deputy Governor replied. "I must find an excuse for the Governor to send me over. Maybe this dispute among the fishermen about how close inshore they can sail their boats is something that we ought to get settled."

"That would, indeed, be useful. And we could spin out the negotiations for a week or so, to give time for you to meet with other members of our little 'European Antiquity Society' – and, of course, enjoy some Japanese hospitality. There's a great deal I would like to show you. For example, one of the Naples artefacts – which I was told came originally from the city of Rome – is a little ivory panel. It's supposed to date from the last days of the ancient Roman Empire, nearly fourteen hundred years ago; and if that is correct it indicates that European art had then reached a higher degree of sophistication than anything that I've seen from more recent centuries. The human figures in it are carved with great realism and accuracy, and convey a range of strong emotions. In some respects it's superior to anything we produced until a couple of hundred years ago."

"What does the panel depict?"

"It shows the son of the Christian god rising from the dead – I expect you know the story. He's in the top right-hand corner, striding vigorously up a hill, or maybe a cloud, with his outstretched hand grasped firmly by the hand of his father emerging out of a cloud. Down below there is an elaborately carved, turreted tomb, surrounded by various characters. In the foreground are three women draped in very elegant robes, whose faces show surprise. One of them has her hand to her mouth. And another character is seated on the plinth of the tomb with one arm raised, presumably telling them that it's empty. Although the scene doesn't use perspective it's very realistically done."

"By a happy coincidence," said the Deputy Governor, "I have planned something for this afternoon which will enable you to make a comparison with the kind of religious art that the Christians are producing today – though it will be painting, not sculpture. In a town on the south side of the estuary there's an important temple, called a 'cathedral', which is being renovated just now. It's situated beside our most important dockyard, and so a lot of the locals are quite prosperous and can afford to pay for the work. But they're getting rid of a lot of the ancient decorations – statues and painted panels – and you can have anything you fancy for a few yuan."

"That sounds most interesting. Very kind of you to arrange it. I shall be fascinated to see how the new decoration differs from the old."

"Not a great deal," said the Deputy Governor. "As you know, religious people are extremely conservative. They believe there is a right way and a wrong way to do everything. It's the same here as it is at home. But I think I do detect the beginning of a change in the work being done by the principal painter working at Rochester – that's the name of the town.

"He's a craftsman in his prime, called Gainsborough, who made his reputation, I'm told, in the restoration of another of these cathedrals, in a town where we've developed the native woollen industry. It's to the north-east of here, a place called Norwich. Anyhow, I've seen two of the paintings he has done for Rochester, and they're much more realistic than the old stuff that's being thrown out. They're more like that ivory panel you described. The fellow may have been influenced by some Eastern paintings that he's seen, not that there are many of those in this benighted colony. Anyhow, you can judge for yourself this afternoon."

We were taken to Rochester in a splendid cutter manned by twelve brawny natives who, when the wind dropped at the end of our journey, produced sweeps to row us over the last couple of miles. The Count and the Deputy Governor sat in the stern along with the helmsman and the young Shantugese Company officer in charge. Lieutenant Hirose and I were seated in the bow. Hirose was very excited because – he confided to me in a whisper – our route was going to take us through the principal anchorage of the Shantungese naval squadron based in Britain.

And so it turned out. Our craft turned out of the Thames Estuary into a tributary called the Medway, passing the fortified town of Sheerness, where a Shantungese frigate lay anchored. It was soon after this that our crew had recourse to the oars, and we were rowed slowly past a succession of desolate, marshy islets until the river began to narrow and we saw ahead on our right a fort of Eastern design, bristling with cannon. Hirose instructed me to stand behind him so that he could make some rapid sketches without being observed from the stern.

As we rounded a bend in the river the masts of several tall ships came into view. They were moored alongside an extensive dockyard that was bustling with activity. "There's a seventy-four – must be the *Ting Yuen* and two fifty-gunners," muttered Hirose. "A couple of fireships would be just what we need to do the trick." He quickly returned his small sketch pad to a coat pocket and pretended to be admiring the view.

We rowed all the way along the dockyard, past the three great ships and several smaller ones, till we came to another tight bend in the river. Ahead of us lay the town of Rochester, and there we found a landing stage. Our walk to the cathedral took less than ten minutes; and beyond it loomed an ancient castle that looked like a smaller version of the Tower of London.

"This temple is looked after by monks, somewhat similar to the Buddhist ones we have in East Asia," said the Deputy Governor as we approached a door of the great, grey building. Our arrival had already been noted, and through the door to greet us came three natives dressed in voluminous black habits, fastened at the waist with white cords. The crowns of their heads were shaven. The man who led the way was plump and elderly, the second was lean and middle-aged, and the third seemed not much more than a youth – possibly about my own age.

"It's the Abbot and the Prior come to greet us," said the Deputy Governor. "That's the head man of the monastery and his second-in-command." He bowed to the approaching monks and they halted and returned the greeting. When the introductions had been made we were conducted inside the building.

As soon as my eyes had become accustomed to the dimness of the light I was astonished at the height of the ceiling, supported by two ranks of massive pillars. We were led up some steps into what appeared to be a separate structure in the centre of the building. It was lined on either side with elaborately carved benches made of some very dark – probably age-darkened – wood; and the Abbot, speaking in Latin with an unfamiliar accent, described it as 'the choir'. Walking through it we turned to the left and halted in front of an elaborate but badly decayed structure which the Abbot told us was the cathedral's most precious possession.

"This is the very tomb of Saint William of Perth," he said, in a tone of great solemnity. "He was a humble baker who had great faith and travelled all the way from Scotland on pilgrimage to the shrine of the holy Saint Thomas Becket in Canterbury, but not far from here he was foully murdered and his body was laid to rest in our cathedral. People came to pray at his grave, and so great was his sanctity that many were healed of their sickness. His fame very quickly spread throughout the whole country, and to this day people still come here to this tomb on pilgrimage, asking the saint to intercede on their behalf. Indeed, tomorrow we are expecting a party of pilgrims from Southampton. And very soon we shall be restoring the decoration of the tomb, to make it worthy once again of the precious remains that lie beneath it."

"How long ago was it that this holy man met his end?" asked the Count.

"This year we celebrate the five hundred and seventy-sixth anniversary of his death," the Abbot replied. "But I know you are interested in the work of restoration that has already been completed; so let me show you our splendid new altarpiece which was unveiled and dedicated by the Bishop only three weeks ago, during our Easter celebrations." (I later learnt from the Count that Easter was the most important Christian festival – although, for reasons he could not discover, the word 'Easter' was actually derived from the name of a goddess of the ancient religion of the island before the Christian religion arrived there.)

We followed the Abbot a short way to the main altar, at the east end of the cathedral. Above it were the three panels of a huge new painting, glowing brightly in an elaborately carved frame that glistened with gold leaf. As we stood before it the Abbot proceeded to explain what the paintings portrayed.

"In the central panel," he said, "you see the coronation of Our Blessed Lady, the Virgin Mary, by the hand of her own son, Jesus Christ, Our Lord." As he spoke the second name he made a rapid movement with his right hand from forehead to chest and shoulder, and his two companions did the same.

The picture showed a sweet-faced, yellow-haired young woman in a red dress and bright blue cloak kneeling on the steps of an elaborate marble throne, on which sat a long-haired, bearded man in a white tunic and dark blue cloak that shimmered with gold leaf ornamentation. He was bending towards her, placing a golden crown on her bowed head. Above the throne, on either side were three chubby, child-like faces, disembodied but sprouting pairs of scarlet wings.

"Was the lapis lazuli you asked us to get from Istanbul used to paint the lady's cloak?" the Deputy Governor enquired.

"It was, indeed," replied the Abbot, "and you can see it again in the right-hand panel. That depicts Saint Andrew, to whom this cathedral is dedicated."

The panel was dominated by the figure of an elderly, white-bearded man in a bright blue robe, who gazed out sternly at the spectators. His left hand was resting on the intersection of two large pieces of timber joined together in the shape of an X. Above his head was the foliage of a tree, on which the artist had clearly expended a great deal of effort to ensure its realistic appearance. And beyond the saint's right shoulder was a glimpse of distant hills that gave some indication of the painter's knowledge of perspective.

"The left-hand panel depicts our other great benefactor, Saint William of Perth," the Abbot continued. With one accord we turned our heads to look at the life-size figure of a bearded, brown-haired man wearing a grey tunic and green stockings. In his right hand he held a long-handled wooden shovel of the kind I have seen bakers use to retrieve loaves from a hot oven, and in his left what looked like the leaf of a palm tree. His rubicund face bore an expression of benevolence, with just the hint of a smile. At that time I had had little acquaintance with paintings, but I thought he was the most lifelike figure I had ever seen portrayed in that medium. Behind him there was a recognizable representation of the local castle.

"It's a very splendid work of art," said the Count.

"It is very different in style from the pictures that were put here in the olden times," said the Abbot, "but now we are living in a very different kind of world. I instructed Thomas, the painter, that he must try to help our people understand that the blessed saints of days gone by were ordinary men and women like themselves, whose achievements they can aspire to imitate. I believe he has had some success in doing that. And the new altarpiece for the Lady Chapel, on which he is presently working, will be even more striking."

I happened to glance at the Prior as the Abbot was speaking, and thought his tight lips and knotted brow indicated strong disapproval; but he said nothing.

"This painter – Thomas Gainsborough I think you said he was called – would he consider undertaking a commission for me?" asked the Deputy Governor. "He shows a skill with faces that makes me think he would be capable of producing a very decent portrait."

"I am sure he would be honoured, Your Excellency. When he has completed the altarpiece I will instruct him to wait on you, if that is your wish," the Abbot replied. "And I understand that your guest," he bowed in the Count's direction, "would be interested in purchasing some of the ancient works for which we no longer have a use. I fear you will find them much eroded by the hand of Time, and dimmed by centuries of smoke from the candles of the faithful." I had noticed that in several parts of the building little clusters of candles were burning. "Brother Matthew will take you to the Crypt, where they are stored, and I think you will find that our excellent Provost, Brother Barnabas, is waiting for your there."

The Deputy Governor expressed our thanks to the Abbot and the Prior, and when farewell bows had been exchanged we followed the young monk back towards the Choir and then down a steep flight of steps. When my eyes had become accustomed to the even dimmer light I was surprised by the elegance of the vaulted roof, supported by massive piers.

We were greeted by a rotund little monk, who seemed eager to show us the array of panels and sculptures stacked against one of the walls. The Count and the Deputy Governor examined each item carefully, questioning Brother Barnabas about its provenance. Eventually the Count selected the pieces that interested him most. There was a large wooden panel, nearly the height of a man and twice as wide, on which the painting was badly obscured but still discernable. It portrayed a man hanging by his arms from a crossbar on a tall post, and on the ground below him a man and women wearing robes that were draped in intricate creases and folds. All three figures had what looked like plates behind their heads, and the heads were inclined at uncomfortable angles. The second chosen object was a stone sculpture, about half life-size and much weathered. It was of a woman holding a baby in her arms, and in spite of the damage the sculptor's skill in portraying a look of tenderness on her face was still evident. The Count's third choice was a large brass plate on which was engraved the full length figures of a man and a woman. He was clad in ancient armour and she in a tall, pointed headdress and a low-cut, tight-waisted dress that suggested a very alluring figure. The plate had, apparently, once covered a grave, and was about three hundred years old.

There was some bargaining with Brother Barnabas about the price, and he eventually settled for a sum which I thought was about the amount the Count would have had to pay in Japan for a good carriage horse. It was arranged that the three objects would be wrapped in sacking and delivered next morning to our boat. We had been invited by the dockyard master to dine with him and spend the night at his house in the neighbouring village of Chatham.

Brother Barnabas and Brother Matthew had to hurry off because they were due to participate in a religious ceremony taking place in the cathedral. As we emerged from the stairway leading down to the crypt we saw some forty or fifty monks taking their places in the area they called the Choir; and by the time we had reached the outer door they had already begun to sing. It was a strange, rhythmic, haunting sound that echoed through the high-ceilinged building, and we paused at the door to listen.

"They are praying to their god," said the Deputy Governor. "They do it seven times a day, beginning with a session in the small hours of the night and ending with one in the evening, before they go to bed. I think they have to keep reminding their god of the need they have for his protection; and the monks do it on behalf of all the other people who couldn't spare the time from their busy lives."

"If they're doing this in temples all over Europa they must believe that their god has very large ears to be able to hear them all at the same time," observed the Count. "But I suppose the same would apply to all religions that have moved away from local gods to universal ones."

"It may be the reason why they attach so much importance to these figures that they call saints," said the Deputy Governor. "They appear to be locally based, and to act as messengers between the people and their god – or rather, gods, because they seem to have three. I haven't been able to work that one out – their belief that they have only one god but he can exist in three different forms, all at the same time."

"Yes, I've been puzzled by that," said the Count. "I want to find out more about their religion because I need it to make sense of their art, about which I'm writing a book." The haunting sound of the singing followed us as we walked away from the great temple.

Next morning, having breakfasted well at the dockyard master's house, Hirose and I hurried back to the jetty in Rochester where the cutter was moored, to take delivery of the Count's purchases. When we arrived the crew, who had been given overnight quarters somewhere else in the dockyard, had not yet appeared. No doubt they had been carousing with some of the locals.

As we stepped down into the boat Hirose remarked, "I see they brought a couple of tarpaulins. We might need those to cover the artwork if it rains." The sky was heavy with clouds. I glanced at the grey tarpaulin lying folded in the bow, and then I looked again, because it seemed to be moving.

"There's something underneath it," I exclaimed. Simultaneously we stepped forward and each took hold of an edge of the heavy material. Hirose nodded to me and together we jerked it upward, to reveal the huddled form of a person dressed in a black habit similar to the monks', but with a piece of sacking covering the head and shoulders. The figure seemed to be asleep, but when the tarpaulin was removed stirred rapidly into waking and twisted around to sit upright. The pale face that stared up at us in alarm was the face of a young woman. Her eyes were bright blue and her eyebrows pale yellow, but her hair was invisible under a tightly-bound white headdress. Putting her hands together in a gesture of supplication, she said something in her native language.

"Do you speak Latin?" I asked in that language, not hopeful of an affirmative reply.

"Yes, yes," she answered eagerly. "Are you Shantungese?"

"No. We're Japanese. What are you doing in this boat?"

"I was hiding and I fell asleep. Please let me stay in the boat. If I have to get out here they'll catch me, now that it's light." Her blue eyes were large and appealing, and a streak of dirt across one pale cheek gave her the appearance of a street urchin – and yet there was refinement in her features and in the timbre of her voice.

"Whom are you running away from?" I asked.

"The nunnery. I don't want to be locked up there. I'm only in it because my father doesn't want to have to pay another dowry if I get married – I'm his third daughter. But I don't want to go on being a nun. Please help me. Please let me go wherever you're going."

I explained what she'd said to Hirose and we discussed what we ought to do while she watched us with anxious eyes. I could see that he was as attracted as I was to the idea of helping a 'damsel in distress'; but we also knew that the Deputy Governor was unlikely to want to be associated with aiding a religious runaway. Glancing down at her once more, her pleading eyes aroused in me a strong desire to know more about her; and I suddenly thought of a strategy.

"The girl must be pretty intelligent to speak such good Latin," I said. "If you want more details about this area, to help you complete your plan of attack, she might be able to answer questions for you. I'd translate. And I think she might be just what Count Furaya needs to help him with this book he's writing. She's bound to know a lot about the Christian religion. If we can smuggle her back to the ship along with the artworks I'll talk to the Count, and maybe he'll agree to take her back with us to Antwerp. But we'll need to keep her out of sight until we get her on board."

I could see that the idea of doing something audacious appealed to the lieutenant's spirit of adventure and, after a moment's hesitation, he agreed to my plan. There was no time to lose, because either the bringers of the artworks or the crewmen might very soon be with us. So I rapidly outlined my plan to the fugitive. As I talked her face was transformed by a smile of gratitude and relief, and I realized that she was actually a beautiful woman. Quickly we wrapped her in the tarpaulin, securing the parcel with a length of cordage that Hirose had discovered. "Untidy bunch of lubbers, these native boatmen," he'd muttered when he found it under one of the thwarts.

We were only just in time. Two pack mules led by a couple of sturdy lads who, I presumed, were employees of the monastery, came clattering along the jetty followed by a monk. And no sooner had we taken on board the three packages than the bleary-eyed crewmen appeared, being berated by the Shantungese officer for their tardiness. I assumed that was what he was saying to them, because I couldn't understand the language. They were followed closely by the Count and the Deputy Governor, and before very long we had cast off. Once again Hirose and I were seated in the bow, with the tarpaulin-wrapped package at our feet. If anyone enquired about it I was ready to say it contained some victuals given us by the dockyard master.

Luckily both wind and tide were in our favour on the return journey. Nevertheless, the young woman must have been incredibly uncomfortable, and I hoped that either the prospect of escape would keep up her spirits or else weariness would allow her to go back to sleep. When eventually we came alongside the brig there were a few anxious moments. While the crewmen, assisted by Japanese sailors, lifted the artworks on to her deck Hirose and I took care of the tarpaulin-wrapped package. I feared that the Count would notice there was a fourth package but he was engaged in a final conversation with the Deputy Governor. From a phrase that I overheard I guessed that they were discussing the forthcoming conflict over the Brunswick succession.

Later, when we stood before the Count on the quarterdeck to confess what we had done I felt less confident of his approval than I had been when the plan first came to me. When I told him how I'd realized that the girl would be able to help him with his book he looked grave, and sceptical, I thought, when I added that she would also be able to assist Lieutenant Hirose with his intelligence gathering. And then he laughed.

"You young fellows are always able to come up with plausible excuses for the mischief you get up to," he said. "But you're right. If the woman is a Christian nun who speaks good Latin, and if she's willing to help me, she could provide just the kind of information I'm looking for, a lot more quickly than having to search through a stack of dusty books. I'll see what she has to say for herself."

So we went below to the tiny cabin allocated to Hirose and me, where we'd taken the girl and unwrapped her. Although exhausted by her journey, she answered the Count's questions promptly and fluently. Her name was Ermyntrude, she said, though the nuns had called her Sister Mary Francis. Her father was a knight in the county of Kent, and he had put her into the nunnery in Rochester against her will because he had married off her two elder sisters and didn't want to have to find a dowry for her. She had been educated by a poor relation, an uncle who was a scholar but was unable to earn a living and had been given a room in her family home, a manor house near the port of Whitstable.

She answered questions with eyes downcast, as the nuns, no doubt, had taught her. But when the Count asked if she would be willing to work for him in Antwerp, helping him to write a book about the art in Christian temples, she looked directly at him, her eyes sparkling with excitement, and answered, "Yes." And when he went on to explain that she would live in his household and would, in addition, be paid four yen a month (which he carefully explained would be equal to six Shantungese yuan) she clapped her hands with unconstrained glee, and then knelt down before him, bowing her head.

The Count permitted a trace of a smile to modify the austerity of his features as he stretched out his hand and raised her up. "You'd better find her something to eat and drink," he said to Hirose and me. "And don't allow her upon deck until we're out to sea. I'll have a word with the captain."

So it was not until the brig had left the land astern (sailing northward to keep well clear of some treacherous quicksands, Hirose informed me) that we took Ermyntrude on deck to breathe fresh air. She had eaten a thick slice of bread and a pickled herring and drunk a beaker of Walloon beer, and the colour had returned very prettily to her cheeks. Standing at the taffrail gazing back at Britain, she suddenly raised both hands to her head and asked, "Can I take off this headdress? I don't want it any more."

"Of course you can," I replied. Immediately she wrenched off the black hood and undid the white covering that was wrapped tightly around her head. With an extravagant wave of her arm she hurled them both into the sea.

"Maybe there's a monkfish down there who will find them," she said, and smiled at me. "I know my hair looks dreadful but it will soon grow again." Her hair had been shorn close to her scalp, which it covered like a silky yellow mat, and although as short as a boy's it somehow didn't look at all masculine.

"Take my scarf to keep your head warm," I said, tugging it out from underneath my jacket. (Kees had advised me to take a scarf on the journey to London, saying that the weather was bound to be cold.) She accepted the dark blue woollen scarf with a smile and wrapped it loosely round her head.

"I don't think I shall ever go back there," she said, nodding towards the receding coastline. "I'm so excited. I want to find out more about the world and all the new ideas we weren't allowed to talk about in the nunnery. I'm so grateful to you both for helping me to escape."

She flashed us both a smile so radiant that, ungraciously, I felt glad that Hirose was unable to talk to her. He was, after all, handsomer and brawnier than me. But I did translate what she'd said, and he returned her smile with a broad grin.

That momentary twinge of jealous protectiveness did, however, give me an idea. I had been wondering how I might continue to see Ermyntrude once she had been taken into the household of the Count. "Perhaps when you're in Antwerp I could help you to learn Japanese," I said.

"Oh yes, I want to do that quickly," she replied. "It will be wonderful if you can help me."

"I look forward to it," I said.

CHAPTER 6

The first few days after our return from Britain were taken up with a flurry of activity related to the Brunswick crisis. I was astonished to discover how many agents – 'spies' I suppose you could call them – Okada had working for him. Their reports kept arriving, a few of them oral and the rest in writing, with a couple penned in a simple code that I had to decipher. They told of troop movements and of messengers being sent from Vienna to Prague and from Dresden to Vienna. Okada read all of them carefully and at the end of each afternoon had a meeting with Governor-General Higashi. He also sent General Kuroki daily summaries of the information received.

After a week had passed the news arrived that Frederick of Brandenburg's troops had entered Brunswick city without encountering any resistance from the Brunswickers, and that Franz had been proclaimed duke. On the following day we heard that Joseph of Austria had issued a proclamation naming Caroline as the rightful duchess, and had received assurances of support from Albrecht of Saxony and Sigismund of Bohemia.

"Frederick has the advantage of being already in possession of the prize," commented Okada as he began preparing his report for the Governor-General, "but if the other three are really able to co-ordinate their efforts he'll have a difficult fight on his hands. The prospect of plunder will fill their ranks with all the ambitious aristocrats in the three duchies, because if Frederick loses they'll certainly be let loose in Brandenburg as well as Brunswick. But it will take them at least a month to put an army in the field – assuming that they're wise enough not to move until everybody is ready."

"Will Frederick be looking for allies?" I asked.

"I expect he's already tried, without success. But they'll underestimate him at their peril. He already has a reputation as a clever general. What he'll have to do is keep his warriors tightly disciplined. They're an arrogant lot who don't like being told what to do, and like all these Europeans they don't understand the importance of time."

When he had finished drafting the report Okada said, "I saw Count Furaya this morning. He asked me to tell you that the young

British woman is ready for her first lesson in Japanese. If you have time this evening after dinner you can call at his house."

I had almost forgotten the offer I'd made to Ermyntrude, and was pleased to hear that she must have sought and obtained the Count's permission to take it up. And so that evening I made my way from the castle (or 'the Steen' as the natives called it) through narrow streets to the ancient house just inside the city wall which Count Furaya had had renovated for himself.

The door was opened by a liveried manservant who seemed to be expecting me, and when I stepped inside the Count himself appeared at the top of a steep stairway and descended to greet me. "The young woman is settling in well," he said, "and I believe she will be extremely useful to me. As well as knowing a lot about her religion she has had an acquaintance with some of the writings of the earlier European civilization. I shall be interested to hear your assessment of her abilities when you have given her a lesson or two."

I said I was proposing initially not to introduce her to reading and writing in Japanese, since that was much more complicated than the European system, but to concentrate on the spoken language. The Count agreed that this would be the best approach and added, "Remember you will be communicating with her in what is her second language, and not her native tongue."

He then led me into what I presumed was the main reception room, saying, "I should like you first to see the pride of my European art collection. I acquired it last year when I was visiting our Governor in Naples."

As we entered a long room, dimly lit by the evening sun, I thought we had disturbed someone already there, seated at the far end on a small dais – a dark-skinned man who was sitting sideways but with his bearded face turned towards us, as though surprised by our entry. Then I realized that I was looking at a bronze statue, the most lifelike I had ever seen.

"That's amazing," I exclaimed as we approached the statue. "You can see the muscles under his skin, and he looks exhausted. How was the sculptor able to do that?"

"Just look under his eye," said the Count, pointing at the statue's head. "Do you see the bruise? The sculptor used a small piece of a different alloy to create it. And look at the drops of 'blood' on his right arm – some kind of red bronze. And if you examine his mouth you can see he's lost a few teeth. It's the figure of a boxer, exhausted at the end of his bout. Those bands wrapped round his wrists and forearms were worn by boxers in the ancient Greek civilization that was even earlier than the Roman one. The Neapolitan who sold me the statue said it must be about two thousand years old. He was selling because he'd lost the fortune left him by his father – a bit of a gambler, I think."

"It really is remarkable," I said, gazing at the weary face and powerful, sagging shoulders. "He looks as if he could get up and walk away."

The Count nodded his head and patted the statue on the shoulder. "I can think of nothing in East Asian art to equal it before the Cultural Reawakening," he said. "It's going to create a sensation in Japan when I take it home. But now you must go and begin your work with the young woman. I should like you to make careful notes of anything she may happen to tell you about the history of her island, as well as her religion, and let me have copies.

He led me along a corridor to a small but high-ceilinged room with two tall, narrow windows looking out on to a courtyard in which I could glimpse some flowering shrubs. Ermyntrude was sitting at a square wooden table and rose to greet us with a curtsey as we entered. Before he left us the Count enjoined her to work hard on learning Japanese, because she then would gain a great deal of pleasure from being able to talk with many more people in her new surroundings.

Ermyntrude needed no encouragement and told me how she had been longing to begin. I was conscious of my own total ignorance of how to teach, having only the examples, both good and bad, of my own former tutors on which to draw. However, I was determined to do my best for her, and to enjoy her company in the process.

When I had ascertained that she was comfortable in her new home and revelling in her freedom with no regrets, we started straight away to explore some basic vocabulary. She had brought a large notebook, in which she began to compile her own dictionary. On the left of the page she wrote down the Latin word and in the centre its Japanese equivalent (in Latin script, of course). Then on the right-hand side she wrote the word in the English language.

After some time I was intrigued to see that a few of the English words were very similar in appearance to the Latin ones, but others bore no resemblance at all. For example, the Latin word ‘animal’ was exactly the same in English whereas ‘corpus’ translated into English as ‘body’. When I pointed this out Ermyntrude said she thought Latin had had some influence on English, maybe because of the way the priests used it when they converted England to Christianity. The English word for a *dead* body was ‘corpse’, she added, and that might have been because the priests had a special responsibility for burying dead bodies.

When she had filled six pages of her notebook I decided she had done enough studying for one day. “Do you miss the people you were living with at the nunnery?” I asked.

“No, not at all,” she replied, shaking her head so vigorously that a lock of yellow hair escaped from the blue linen wimple that covered her head and neck. “Well… maybe there was one girl that I liked, called Sister Edith; but we hardly ever had a chance to talk to each other. We only once had a really good conversation. It was when we were working together in the garden, picking peas. But an older nun, called Sister Mary Benedict, was working with us and she told the Abbess that we’d been talking. She was scheming to get the job of prioress because it had just come vacant – and later on she did get it. Anyhow, after that the Abbess made sure that Sister Edith and I didn’t get any more chances to talk. They were a pretty miserable lot; but then half of them didn’t really want to be there, and you couldn’t blame them.”

“Were many of them there because, like you, their families didn’t want the expense of a marriage dowry?”

To my surprise Ermyntrude’s cheeks turned bright red, and she hesitated for several seconds before replying. “Yes… yes, there were some like that,” she stammered. “But I’m afraid what I told you wasn’t really true. I wasn’t forced to take the veil. In fact, my father wasn’t really in favour of it. I was the one who made the decision to be a nun. But I was only sixteen and I didn’t really understand what I was doing.”

“But why did you tell me the” – I was about to say “lie” but thought better of it – “story about the dowry?”

"I thought you would be more sympathetic if you thought I'd been forced into the nunnery against my will, and I wanted to be sure you'd help me to escape. The real story was too complicated to explain in just a minute or two. Was that wrong of me?"

"No, it wasn't," I replied, "but I'd like to hear the real story."

Her blue eyes, which had been looking anxiously into mine, brightened into a smile. "I'll try to tell you," she said, "even though I don't completely understand it all myself. It all started just after my sixteenth birthday, when these two friars came to preach at Whitstable. Friars are like monks only they travel around more, preaching and teaching. Brother John and Brother Charles were quite famous – they still are – and they're unusual because they actually are brothers, from the same family. Brother Charles is a good singer and he makes up religious songs and teaches people to sing them at their meetings, while Brother John is very good at preaching. They travel all over the country telling people that they've got to be more serious about their religion if they want to go to Heaven when they die."

"The priests must be very pleased to have their help," I said.

"Not all of them are," she replied. "I suppose it's because when people start getting serious about religion they also start asking questions they hadn't thought about before, and most of the priests think ordinary people ought not to ask questions. They should just do as they're told.

"One of Brother John's favourite quotations from the Bible – that's our holy book – was, 'Be you also perfect, as your Father in Heaven is perfect.' But when I was little I was taught that I couldn't be perfect, because of what the first woman, called Eve, had done when God created the world. However, I was told that when I did do something wrong I just had to confess it to a priest and do my penance, and then God would forgive me and everything would be all right – until the next time. But Brother John taught us that if we really tried hard to follow Jesus Christ God would help us to get better and better so that, even before we died we could be living like Jesus, in perfect harmony with God. I thought that was for me. I could be a saint."

"So to do that you had to become a nun?" I asked.

"Not exactly. Brother John said people who weren't in holy orders could still live their lives like Jesus, but that would involve doing a lot of very difficult things. They would have to give all their possessions to the poor (though if they were married they could keep enough to support their families) and spend a lot of their time praying and visiting the sick and telling other people to repent of their sins; and above all they mustn't love anything or anybody more than they loved God. I could see straight away that for a woman it would be almost impossible to do all that unless she became a nun."

"And was that when you decided to go into the nunnery?"

"Yes, but first I had long arguments with my father and mother. They brought in the parish priest and he told me I could still be good and go to Heaven even if I lived an ordinary life. But I didn't want to be ordinary: I wanted to be somebody special. So eventually they gave in and let me become a nun."

"When did you change your mind?" I asked.

"I think it began quite early on, and it was all because the Abbess was worried that I was too enthusiastic about the teachings of Brother John. You see, he belongs to an order of friars called the Franciscans – after a saint who lived about five hundred years ago. But our abbey was Cistercian. The nuns who founded it escaped to England from France when the Mongols invaded – which was also about five hundred years ago. And our Abbess wasn't happy with some of the Franciscans' ideas, especially in the way that Brother John was teaching them. She thought they were dangerous because they might make people discontented with the Church – 'and the Church is our one and only doorway to salvation', she told me.

"Because I could speak good Latin she gave me a job in the library, writing out copies of the ancient books to send to other religious houses and schools. She thought it would help me to understand the true doctrines of the Church."

"And did it?"

"Yes, but not in the way the Abbess thought it would. The senior scribe was Sister Catherine, and she taught me how to do the work. There were just the two of us, I suppose because not many girls learn to read and write and even fewer learn Latin. Copying is mostly done by monks; but our library came with the nuns from France all those hundreds of years ago, and they wanted to keep up the tradition. Religious people are like that. Anyhow, around the end of my first year Sister Catherine fell ill. It was winter and she had to stay in the infirmary for a couple of months; so I was left on my own. I started looking in some of the old books and then I spent more and more of my time reading. Sister Catherine had taught me well and I was very quick at copying – much quicker than she had been, in recent years, anyhow, because her fingers were stiff, poor old dear. But it meant that the Abbess didn't realize I was spending a lot of my time reading."

"Did the reading change the way you were thinking?"

"Not at first; but then I started searching in a cupboard full of old books that looked as if they hadn't been touched for centuries, and I found some that were very different from the stuff I'd been copying. Some of them had been written more than a thousand years ago – the originals, that is. I suppose they must have been copied lots of times.

"There was one book by a man called Eusebius that was the life story of the great Roman Emperor Constantine. He was the first emperor to be a Christian, and this man Eusebius seems to have actually known him. It was a fascinating book, but what really surprised me was the stories he told about how some of the great doctrines of the Church – the things that Christians have to believe – were actually agreed on. Do you know about them?"

"Not very much," I replied, "but I have begun finding out – like when I looked at pictures in the temple at Rochester."

"Well, there's one very important doctrine about how there is only one god but he is actually three people, the Father, the Son and the Holy Ghost. It seems that in Constantine's time, which was about three hundred years after Christianity began, some Christians believed that the Son, Jesus, had been created by the Father and so was separate from him and not really a god. The people who believed that, including lots of bishops, were called Arians and they had huge arguments with the other Christians. Sometimes there were riots in the cities and people actually killed each other.

"Anyhow, Constantine wanted the religious leaders to get together and decide what should be the official doctrine, and he brought them from different parts of the Roman Empire for a Council at a place called Nicaea. They had a lot of trouble agreeing about the words in a statement – what the Church calls a 'creed'. But Constantine seems to have bullied all but two of them – there were about three hundred altogether – into signing up to the really important sentence in the creed."

"Do you remember what that was?"

"We had to repeat it every day in the nunnery. It says that Jesus is the only-begotten son of god, begotten not created, and he is of one substance with his Father. That's the important bit, the 'one substance'. After the bishops had all agreed to it Constantine organized a big banquet for them, and sent each of them home with a personal present. And about seven months later he killed his own son and his sister's stepson, and then his wife, because he believed they were plotting against him – which they may well have been. But I was really shocked when I discovered that these were the kind of people who had decided what should be the 'eternal truths' that I'd been taught to believe. And that was just one example of things that I found written in those old books. Of course, the people who wrote them always seemed to think it was God who had arranged what the outcome was going to be."

"And was that when you decided you wanted to get out of the nunnery?"

"No. It didn't happen at once. I can't really remember exactly when I made that decision. It was a gradual process going on in my mind, I suppose. If you've always been taught that you'll go to Hell if you don't believe exactly what the Church tells you to believe it's not easy to start thinking for yourself."

"I'm sure it can't be easy," I said, trying to imagine how I would have acted if I'd been brought up to believe in primitive superstitions. For some reason I remembered the fear I had seen on the faces of two elderly peasants when their Shinto shrine was blown over in a storm not far from where I grew up as a boy.

"It was easier when I found some copies of books that were even older than the one by Eusebius. They must have been written by Romans who lived before the Church took over everything. I was very surprised to find them in the library. Maybe some rich man, some lord or duke, left his collection of books to the nunnery hundreds of years ago and nobody really bothered to look at them.

"But it wasn't really reading books that made up my mind for me: it was starting to think for myself. That was something I hadn't thought was possible, until I found out that long ago people held different opinions and nobody had any real evidence to prove which one was right. So I started thinking about the words I had to sing in the chapel every day. They said that God had made everybody and he loved everybody; and yet most people were going to end up in a horrible place called Hell, apart from some of the ones who were lucky enough to be born in places where they would be told that God had sent his son – who was actually himself – to earth to save them. But they would only be saved from Hell if they believed the people who were telling them that that was really what had happened. When I tried to think about it as if I'd never heard it before it just didn't make sense. Either this god was actually very cruel – and I'd read that the old Romans believed that their gods were often cruel – or else, if he really did love people, he wasn't capable of working out a better way to make sure they would all escape going to the Hell that he had made for them. And he must have made it, because we sang every day that 'without him nothing was made that was made'."

"So did you come to the conclusion that your god must be both cruel and stupid?" I asked.

"No, I didn't. Jesus, the man who was supposed to be god come to earth as his own son, definitely wasn't cruel, if all the things written about him are true. So I guessed that maybe he'd just been mistaken in thinking there was a god who was his father. After all, everyone else in those days believed there was a god who was going to send someone to save them from the Romans, who had taken over their country; so maybe they'd persuaded him that he was the one. He seems to have been the kind of preacher who could make people want to do what he told them, a bit like the way Brother John's preaching made me want to go into the nunnery."

I looked into Ermyntrude's face, which was pinker and more attractively rounded than when I first met her, and marvelled at the way in which her blue eyes seemed to sparkle with energy as she talked. How much intelligence and how much courage she must have needed to reject those deeply ingrained beliefs of everyone else around her, I reflected. "Does that mean you decided there might not be a god up there, after all?" I asked.

"Yes, or if there was he was too far away to be bothered about what I was thinking. Saying prayers to him seven times a day was a terrible waste of effort. There had to be more useful things to do – and things that were more fun. So I made up my mind to get out; but if you hadn't come along I might not have succeeded."

"Oh, I'm sure you would have found a way," I said; but I was secretly pleased to be given the credit for having rescued her. And I wanted now to find out what kind of person she really was, for she seemed to epitomise something that I and my student friends in Sendai had often argued about. All but a couple of us had come to the conclusion that the Tsunami of Reason need not be confined to East Asia, but could benefit the whole of mankind – including, of course, the ignorant and superstitious peasants of our own country, once they had been educated. Here, in Ermyntrude, I could see the living proof of that belief.

A discreet tap on the open door of the room made us turn our heads and an elderly European manservant bowed low and reminded me, in halting Japanese, that the hour of curfew was approaching. I thanked him and prepared to leave. Ermyntrude, to my surprise, made me a little curtsey and said how much she had enjoyed the lesson. I had greatly enjoyed my conversation with her, I said; and we arranged to meet again in two days' time.

Walking rapidly back to the Steen through the darkening streets I experienced a mixture of emotions. There was a sense of exhilaration at having been able to engage in an equal relationship with a woman for the very first time. (My encounter with the Duchess was in a different category, being something out of the ordinary.) But I also felt ambivalent about the strong physical desire that Ermyntrude had aroused in me. It might be easy enough to exploit her gratitude and her vulnerability, and yet that was something I didn't want to do. But I knew I could never be content with just the enjoyment of her intelligent conversation. The Duchess had sharpened my appetite for all the other delights of an intimate relationship. And beyond that I sensed the stirring of emotions that were unfamiliar to me – a desire to protect, an urge to confide, a longing to be longed form.

I was confused, but I was happy.

CHAPTER 7

"Find out from the Duchess just how big is the extent of her ambitions, and let me know as quickly as you can." That was Okada's final instruction to me before I began my journey to Holstein. And he added: "If you have to give her some fun in the process I'm sure it won't be a hardship for you. But get me the information – it's important."

I had been chosen to act as his observer and liaison with the Duchess as the Brunswick crisis approached its climax. Accompanying me to Holstein would be a veteran sergeant of the Flemish Regiment of Native Infantry, Herman Smet, who spoke good German and Japanese, and Kees Zalm, the Dutch clerk who shared my office. It would be the task of Kees to carry back my message orally, since Okada did not want to risk committing to paper something that would reveal the nature of his own interest in Sophia's plans.

Our journey on a Company brig to Bremen took longer than expected because of a contrary wind, and when we arrived we found that the Duchess and the army she had been assembling had already departed southward. And there were rumours on every tongue about an impending clash between the forces of Frederick and Joseph, somewhere to the south-east. So we hired a river-boat and set off upstream on the River Weser, which was bristling with small craft carrying supplies to the army or returning empty to pick up fresh loads.

As we sailed slowly upstream against the current I had time to become anxious about my impending encounter with the Duchess. She had sent me a letter a week earlier, delivered by the messenger who carried her official correspondence to Okada. In it she had said that the memory of our 'time together' had revived her when she was exhausted by all the endless preparations for the crisis ahead. It was a short letter ending with the sentence: "When the victory is ours and I am ruling triumphantly in Brunswick you must come and visit me again."

I had replied, describing my visit to Britain and Count Furaya's enthusiasm for antiquities, but making no reference either to the activities of Lieutenant Hirose or to my encounter with Ermyntrude. By that time I knew that Okada had decided to send me to liaise with her, and so I was able to write enthusiastically about the prospect of very soon being with her once again. But my real feelings were much more ambivalent. Another opportunity to enjoy the sensual delights of Sophia's body was extremely desirable, but now my desire was tinged with an illogical suggestion of guilt. There was absolutely no reason to feel that I had some kind of bond with Ermyntrude that constrained my relationships with other women, and yet I did.

My half-dozen meetings with the British girl had been very correct, involving not even a suggestion of physical contact. Nevertheless, the feeling of intimacy had grown stronger at every encounter. When Ermyntrude laughed the sparkle in her eyes seemed to suggest that the joke, whatever it might be, was something only she and I could share. When she talked about her childhood she was completely candid and unrestrained. And increasingly I found myself telling her about things that had happened when I was growing up in Japan, while she questioned me eagerly about the details. We had known each other for just a month but already I seemed to be closer to her than I had ever been to anyone else. And that now seemed more important to me than even the prospect of another encounter with the enchantingly voluptuous Duchess.

I had no time for any further reflections once we arrived at the landing stage in Minden. It was thronged with bizarrely accoutred soldiers, bristling with weaponry, and sweating porters loading barrels and boxes on to a string of barges. We had considerable difficulty finding anyone who could tell us where the Duchess was quartered, but eventually a man with an ostrich plume in his bonnet, who spoke to me in Latin, directed us to the Rathaus which, Sergeant Smet informed me, was the town hall.

The Duchess greeted us warmly, proferring me her hand to kiss. She was surrounded by clerks and officers, only one of whom she introduced. He was the tall, yellow-bearded Oldenburg, commander of the army, who remembered our meeting in Hamburg. "My daughter Frederika greatly enjoyed your company at supper," he said. "I believe she taught you to dance."

"She was an excellent teacher, sir," I replied.

"Well, you will soon have an opportunity to see us dancing to a different kind of tune – the blast of the trumpets and the roar of the guns," he said.

"It's a dance at the end of which you're going to make your partners all fall down," said the Duchess, and he laughed appreciatively. A young officer was then instructed to find accommodation for us in a nearby house, and to return there after two hours to conduct me to her own lodgings, where I was invited to have supper.

As we lay side by side on the huge Western-style bed with posts at its corners and a canopy overhead, sweat drying on our temporarily exhausted bodies, the Duchess reached out a hand to stroke my cheek and remarked, "You have forgotten nothing that I taught you. Have you been practising with someone else?"

"No," I replied truthfully, "but I have been remembering again and again every moment that we enjoyed together." Less truthfully, I added, "And I've been longing for the time when we could be together again."

"You're a sweet boy," she said, and then she gave a deep sigh. "And you're still at the beginning. It's the best time, when everything is new and surprising and – if you're lucky – so much better than you thought it was going to be. But you can never go back there; so enjoy it while you can."

"For me it's so good because you've made it good," I replied. Then, remembering Okada's instructions, I asked, "Shall we do it again to celebrate your victory? How soon do you think that will be?"

"Very soon now, I hope." She turned on her side and began to stroke my chest. "We heard this afternoon that Frederick's battle has begun somewhere near Brunswick city. The army will start moving eastward at dawn tomorrow and I will follow later in the morning. When he has won his battle – because I think he will win even though he is outnumbered – then we'll not give him a moment to catch his breath. We'll push him back to where he came from, and beyond."

"Beyond? Where would he go?"

"To take refuge with the Slavs, or the Scandinavians, if he can run fast enough. I don't care where he goes provided he leaves his treasury behind."

"You mean that you'll invade Brandenburg if you defeat him?" I tried to sound only half-interested.

"Of course I shall. I need to give you some lessons about the body politic as well as the body beautiful," she replied, smiling down at me, and her fingers moved towards my groin. "When you win a victory you must press your advantage. Otherwise you may find that in a few years you have to fight the battle all over again. If I destroy Frederick's army… when I destroy Frederick's army I'm not going to let him run back to Berlin and start creating a new one."

"So you will annex Brandenburg as well as Brunswick? That will be magnificent. You will be a Grand Duchess at the very least."

She laughed, and her eyes were sparkling as she gazed down into mine. "My son will be a king," she said, "the King of the German people. We can't go on for ever with this patchwork of principalities that grew out of our fathers' struggle to be rid of the Empire and its pashas. There are still some pashas oppressing the south and the west, as well as that so-called Sultan in Augsburg, pretending that his empire still exists. Your Company goes along with that pretence, doesn't it?"

"Yes, I believe we send him some kind of nominal tribute every year."

"His time will come; but first we've got to get rid of those pashas lording it over Lorraine and Franconia and Swabia. That's only going to happen if the Germans are united under one ruler, with one army. Joseph of Austria says he wants to revive the old Holy Roman Empire, but that so-called empire wasn't able to resist the Mongols, because it wasn't an empire: it wasn't united. Every duke and count and baron wanted to be his own master and in the end the Mongols destroyed them all. And when the Mongols left it began all over again, with every warlord grabbing a bit of territory for himself. I've heard they even tried to start the Empire again at that time, with a Frenchman as the emperor, because the French were the first to get rid of the Mongols. And then Joseph's ancestors had the title for awhile, but that didn't do them much good when the Turks came. They couldn't stop fighting each other for long enough to hold back the invaders. And if the Turks hadn't started fighting among themselves they might still be ruling over the whole of Europa. What we need is a Kingdom of the Germans, and before this month is out I shall have begun to create it."

She withdrew her hand from my body and sat upright on the bed. "I shall follow the army at about seven o'clock tomorrow morning," she said. "You can come with me and watch history being made; but now we must both get some sleep. Who knows when we shall next have an opportunity?"

I set out next day with the Duchess in her sturdy four-horse coach, accompanied by Gretchen, her lady-in-waiting, and Wolfgang Steinberg, her secretary. Sergeant Smet travelled behind, on the luggage wagon. And Kees departed down river, ostensibly to carry the news to Okada that the army of Holstein was moving to engage the enemy, but actually to convey to him the conversation that I had had with the Duchess.

The road on which we travelled followed the river valley through a region of hills, some of them thickly forested, and farmland that looked fertile. In the numerous villages through which we passed the inhabitants stayed indoors, and from time to time I saw anxious faces peering through windows. When I remarked on it the Duchess said, "People are always frightened when an army passes by – and with good reason. But I have given strict instructions that there must be no looting. Oldenburg will hang any man caught doing it. These people are our subjects now, and we want them not to be afraid of us."

On the second night we halted in a town called Hamelin. It was a picturesque place with some fine houses, on the walls of which inscriptions were printed boldly in the local language. The Duchess told me they were supposed to be wise and witty sayings, but the wit was not always easy to discern. The townspeople, she said, also kept alive an ancient legend about a piper wearing multi-coloured clothes who had once rid the town of a plague of rats; and then, when the council hadn't given him the money they'd promised, he had used his magical piping to lure away all their children.

The Duchess was able to spend that night in a relatively palatial house, lent to her by one of the leading citizens. When the military leaders, still anxiously awaiting news of Frederick's movements, had retired to their own quarters I was once again invited to come to her bed. She was in a restless, excited mood and our vigorous coupling seemed to calm her. When she finally patted my buttocks and told me it was time for me to leave I had scarcely finished fastening my breeches before her eyelids were lowered in sleep.

Early next morning there was great excitement. A messenger had ridden through the night with the news that on the previous day Frederick had met and defeated the army of Albrecht, Duke of Saxony, at a place called Wolfenbuttel. But he was now about to be assailed from the south-west by Archduke Joseph, whose army had marched through southern Saxony, bringing with it reinforcements from the Duke of Bohemia. A second battle must be imminent.

"It's all going as we would wish it to," said the Duchess when she heard the news. "I hope that Frederick took heavy casualties." The messenger said he had heard that the Saxons had put up a stubborn resistance before being forced to retreat.

"Oldenburg, your predictions were exactly right," said the Duchess, looking up approvingly at her tall general, who bowed his head gravely in acknowledgement. "Now we can move on as planned to Hildesheim, and hope that by the time we get there Joseph will have done most of our work for us."

So the army moved on again, this time on a more difficult road that wound through hilly country away from the river valley. On the first day Secretary Steinberg kept the Duchess occupied dealing with the contents of a batch of letters delivered to him by a courier at Hamelin. That evening we lodged in a small village inn while the army camped on surrounding hillsides. Fortunately the weather was dry and warm. There was little privacy in our cramped surroundings and I was not invited to join the Duchess at bedtime.

As we moved on next day there was a mounting sense of anticipation. On several occasions officers rode back to inform the Duchess of rumours about a battle to the east, but none of these stories was confirmed. It was not until mid-afternoon, when we were approaching the town of Hildesheim, that firm intelligence was received. A troop of light cavalry had been dispatched by Oldenburg to scout beyond the horizon and eventually one of them came riding back, urging on his weary horse as he approached the coach across a field that bordered the road. Oldenburg, who was then riding alongside us, ordered the coach to stop and wait for the returning scout.

As I clambered down from the coach, glad to be able to stretch my legs, I was struck by the unusual costume worn by the approaching rider. His calf-length blue coat was fastened down the front with large white metal buttons, on either side of which were thick bands of silver braid that stretched right across his chest. On his head he wore a bright red cap, dangling down at one side over a thick turned-back brim of black fur, and surmounted in front by a white plume of egret's feathers. In the red and yellow sash around his waist he carried a couple of long-barrelled pistols and a curved sword hung at his side.

"What uniform is that?" I asked Gretchen.

"Oh, he's a Magyar," she replied. "The Duchess hired a troop of them last year. They're very good horsemen and they know how to scout without getting caught by the enemy."

The Magyar dismounted, bowed low to the Duchess and made his report to Oldenburg in the German language. We were able to hear what he said, and Gretchen translated for me in a low voice. "He says there is a big battle raging somewhere near the town of Salzgitter. He could hear a lot of cannon-fire and musketry and then he was able to see the smoke. There was so much smoke that it had to be the two main armies; but he didn't go closer because he wanted to come back quickly and report."

The Duchess said something to Steinberg, who produced a purse from under his cloak and gave the cavalryman a gold coin. She had a brief discussion with Oldenburg, who called for his horse, and then she returned to the coach. "The army will rest overnight in Hildesheim and have a really good meal. Then at first light tomorrow we'll set off in search of whoever wins that battle," she told me.

"Do you think it will be Frederick?" I asked.

"I do," she replied. "Joseph may be thirty years younger, but he's indecisive and he's inexperienced. He'll never make a great commander. I predict that by tomorrow he'll be running back into Saxony with whatever remains of his army."

On the following day we learned that her prediction had been right.

CHAPTER 8

It was two days before the Duchess and her army finally caught up with Frederick of Brandenburg. In the ancient town of Hildesheim we had slept in a house below the tower of a Christian temple – called a cathedral or, in the local language, 'Dom' – which Gretchen told me was nine hundred years old. Next morning extra rations were distributed to the soldiers before they set out on their march to what, it was assumed, would be an early battle.

During the first day reports began coming in that Frederick had, indeed, defeated his opponents. The first scouts to return said that the battle was still raging, but later information suggested that it had ended before sunset with the rout of Joseph's forces. Two scouts brought back with them a local merchant who claimed to have witnessed the fighting, some of which had taken place in the village of Henneckenrode. The merchant said he had been in the village inn when a troop of Brandenburg horse had charged and scattered a company of Austrian infantry who had just arrived there. That had been at about five o'clock in the afternoon and he had heard the sound of gunfire for about another two hours, gradually becoming more distant. He had stayed in the inn overnight and had been intercepted by the Magyars on his way to Brunswick early in the morning. All the Brandenburg troops seemed to have moved on to the south he said, although he had seen one cart containing wounded men going back to the city.

At this news Oldenburg became very excited and ordered another troop of Magyars to ride with all speed to discover the whereabouts of the enemy. "Joseph will almost certainly have retreated along the Nette towards Bockenem, and Frederick will be in hot pursuit," the Duchess informed me, as the carriage began to move. "If we can catch up with him today he'll have to stand and fight. He'll have no room to manoeuvre."

By around midday we came to what had clearly been the site of a significant battle. It looked as if the wounded had already been removed, for none could be seen near the road, but from the coach window I did have glimpses of several dead bodies, partly stripped of their clothing – no doubt by the local peasants, who would have fled at our approach. But we pressed on at our lumbering pace without pausing.

A little later Oldenburg rode back to the coach to bring the Duchess up to date with the latest intelligence. The visual evidence suggested there had been two major encounters, he said. The second, at the village of Schleweke, through which we had just passed, had probably been a rearguard action to enable the bulk of Joseph's army to escape to the south. The first of the Holstein cavalry were already entering the small town of Bockenem and no doubt they would find wounded men left behind there who could be questioned.

Oldenburg's surmise was correct and there were several hundred wounded men in the town, both Brandenburgers and Austrians. Among those who were questioned no two had seen exactly the same view of the battle, and the picture that emerged was confused. However, it seemed that Joseph had advanced boldly, believing part of Frederick's army must be still engaged with the Saxons, and at the Henneckenrode river crossing Frederick had hit him with a surprise flank attack, routing his best troops. The rest of the Austrians had retreated in good order but were being hotly pursued.

A Brunswick knight, one of the party supporting the claim of Frederick's son-in-law, who had joined with the Brandenburg army, was among the wounded. When questioned he had apparently decided it would be prudent to change sides and had been very helpful with his answers. According to him Frederick had received news only as the battle was beginning that the Duchess had arrived at Hamelin with an army. Although surprised, he had assumed that she must have entered into a secret alliance with Joseph, and that when she heard of Joseph's defeat she would take herself swiftly back to Holstein.

"So he will be surprised to find us waiting for him when he makes his way back," said the Duchess when Oldenburg had finished telling her the news, standing by the coach in Bockenem town square.

"Just so, Your Grace," Oldenburg replied. "If we take up our position in the village of Bornum, just to the south of here, we will bar his way back. I'm sure he'll think we're either retreating or heading for Brunswick city, and he'll want to get there before us."

It was decided that the army would move south immediately and encamp overnight in positions ready for battle the next day. Bornum was situated near where the road from the south emerged from between the hills and there was an area of comparatively flat and unwooded land which would allow the cavalry to manoeuvre. When we arrived there the army was drawn up in a huge semicircle so that the Duchess would be able to address her troops – though I guessed that only those nearest the front would be able to hear what she was saying.

It was the first time that I had been able to see all or, indeed, even a substantial part of the force, because for the whole of the journey the Duchess's entourage had been travelling at the rear of the column. Now, standing behind the small platform of planks stretched across upturned barrels, which had been erected to make her more visible from a distance, I was able to see all the different units, with the exception of the artillery, which was halted behind us in a long procession, stretching back through the village.

To my left in the semicircle I could see a small group of Magyar horsemen, the majority of whose comrades must still have been engaged in their scouting activities. Next to them was a regiment of cavalry drawn up in ordered ranks and wearing Eastern-style uniforms, with gleaming steel cuirasses and helmets. I guessed they were the Duchess's Lifeguards whom I had seen in Hamburg, and they appeared to number about five hundred.

To identify the other formations I had to rely on Gretchen, who was standing beside me a little way behind the Duchess's platform. We had ample time to survey the scene during the formalities that followed.

Beside the Lifeguards another dismounted cavalry formation was drawn up, but it was not nearly so uniform in appearance nor so orderly in its ranks. Every man seemed to be dressed in his own fashion, and all were armoured to some degree, ranging from a simple breastplate over a leather tunic to elaborate suits of half or three-quarters complete steel armour. They were equipped with lances, swords of various kinds and pistols. Gretchen told me they were knights and men-at-arms from the County of Oldenburg; and they also numbered around five hundred.

The formation of foot soldiers standing next to them must have been three times their number, but were markedly inferior in weapons and equipment. The foremost ranks had helmets and breastplates, and were armed with long pikes. Behind them I could see little in the way of armour and the men were equipped with poleaxes, short spears or scythe-blades mounted vertically on staves. They were the Oldenburg 'levies', men conscripted from their farms to follow their landlords into battle.

Flanking them, however, was a body several hundred strong that looked more formidable. Uniformly dressed in buff coats, grey woollen trousers and blackened steel helmets, they were armed with muskets. I noted that while the front few ranks had Eastern-style flintlocks those behind carried matchlocks of the kind that went out of use in East Asia over a century ago. Gretchen told me that these were the Bremen Guildsmen, who would be fighting in conjunction with the Oldenburg levies. The next formation looked similar to the Oldenburg levies but was not quite so large. It was made up of the levies mustered by Count Albrecht von Meldorf, Gretchen informed me. But it was flanked by a band of musketeers that was larger and better equipped than the men of Bremen. Their flag was bright red with a white, three-towered castle in the centre, and they were the Guildsmen of Hamburg.

In the centre of the semicircle were two battalions in Eastern-style uniforms and equipment who could, from their appearance, have been a regiment of the Company's native infantry, except that their tunics were light blue instead of red. "Those are the Duchess's Foot Guards," said Gretchen. "The second battalion was formed only a month ago. You can their colonel, Yamada, standing with the big black horse. He used to be an officer in your Company's army."

Next to the Guards stood a strangely attired company of predominantly bearded warriors whose principal armament appeared to be broadswords and small round shields, although I also noticed pistol-butts protruding from some of their belts. They were dressed in what seemed to be long-skirted robes made from geometrically patterned material, and on their bearded heads they wore bonnets from which feathers protruded.

"Where do those fierce-looking fellows come from?" I asked.

"They're mercenaries from the northern part of Britain," Gretchen replied. "They're known as 'Lord Cameron's Scots' and they were employed by Duke Gerhart of Mecklenburg, but the Duchess bought them from him just a few weeks ago. They do have a reputation for being very fierce."

Beside the Scotsmen stood another formation of levies, mustered by the Counts of Ratzeburg and Eutin and supported by the Guildsmen of Lübeck. Beyond them were three detachments of armoured cavalrymen, each formation somewhat smaller than the array that followed the banner of Oldenburg. These, Gretchen told me, were the knights and men-at-arms mustered by the Counts of Meldorf, Ratzeburg and Eutin.

At the very end of the semicircle stood one more band of armoured riders, numbering about two hundred. They were Brunswickers who had already pledged their allegiance to the Duchess and her son, Otto. Gretchen pointed out their leader, a huge man in full armour standing by his equally huge grey horse. His name was Count Ulrich von Weserbergland.

"Where are the artillerymen?" I asked.

"Oh, the guns are still coming up. They were at the end of the column," Gretchen replied. "And anyhow they wouldn't understand much of what's going on. They're nearly all mercenaries from the Taiwanese territory of Brest. I think a lot of Frederick's gunners come from the same place. They work for some of the pashas, too. They're mostly AisEuropeans, you know, and the job of handling big guns seems to have been passed down in their families for generations. I've heard that it was the Taiwanese who first brought guns to Europa, and they helped the Duke of Brittany to break free from the Sultan, and so he gave them the port of Brest, where they set up their factory."

"I expect I shall be seeing them later on," I said. "How many guns does the Duchess have?"

"Fourteen big ones and twelve small ones – that's not counting the guns in her castles, of course. The Duchess thinks they're important, but I know that a lot of the warriors don't like them, and think they're only useful for sieges. They take a lot of time to move. But look, I think the Duchess is going to make a speech."

Sophia had put on a light blue Guards officer's tunic over her grey riding habit. As she stepped to the centre of the makeshift platform she raised her right hand above her head and the huge assembly fell quiet. Then she began to speak, clearly and strongly, in the German language. In a subdued voice Gretchen translated for me into Latin, often hesitating and, no doubt, missing out phrases that weren't essential; but she very ably gave me the gist of what was being said, and later that night I wrote it down so that I could remember it for Okada.

Tomorrow, the Duchess told the assembled soldiers, would be a decisive day, not only for the Duchy of Brunswick but for all the German people. Tomorrow they would be fighting not just to establish the rightful claim of Otto, her son and heir, to the dukedom. Tomorrow they would be taking the first step on a road that would lead to the unity of the German people and an end to the quarrels that divided them and weakened them in the face of their enemies. Tomorrow, when the usurper had been cast down, that unification would begin with the coming together of the peoples of Brunswick and Holstein; and the way would be open for others to rally behind their triumphant banner. Tomorrow the light would begin to shine through the clouds for those German people who were still groaning under the yoke of heathen oppressors. Tomorrow, with the help of God, the drumbeats of victory would signal the start of a new era for all Christian people in the German lands. By rallying behind a single banner they would gain the strength to vanquish all their foes. Tomorrow that banner would be raised in triumph, and behind it the German people would begin to march, however long the road might be, to their own kingdom, cleansed of all heathen oppressors, where they could live together in security and peace.

When the Duchess stopped speaking there was a huge cheer that rippled backwards from the foremost ranks, who would have heard clearly what she said, to the men at the rear, who doubtless were later told the content of her speech. I noticed that the Magyars and the Scots, most of whom wouldn't have understood a word, joined in at the end by brandishing their weapons above their heads.

I had assumed that when the Duchess spoke of a "triumphant banner" she was talking figuratively, but I now discovered that she had given substance to her words. From the street behind us a strange vehicle approached, drawn by two black horses. It was a kind of rectangular cart on four wheels, from the centre of which arose a flagstaff like the mast of a ship, secured by guy ropes to the four corners of the cart. From the pole flew a huge flag, permanently displayed outward by being attached at the top to a rigid crossbar fixed to the head of the staff. The flag bore a black cross with a white border on a scarlet field.

"It's the caroccio," Gretchen exclaimed, "but I've never seen that flag before. It must have been what the Duchess was planning with Count Dietrich and Secretary Steinberg. It's a flag for everyone, not just Holsteiners." Her eyes were shining and I could see that she shared in the enthusiasm kindled by Sophia's speech.

As the caroccio came to a halt in the space in front of the platform a little procession of priests made its way forward, led by a man in a loose white robe carrying a silver cross on the end of a long pole. The most important figure among them appeared to be a man wearing a richly embroidered cape and a high, pointed hat. "That's the Bishop of Hildesheim," Gretchen told me. "He's going to consecrate the flag."

A long series of religious rituals then began. I hesitated to question Gretchen about their meaning because she was clearly caught up in the mood of devotion and I didn't wish to offend her. At one stage in the proceedings the priests drank ceremonially from large cups, held for them by young lads in white capes. And then I saw the Duchess and Count Dietrich kneel down in front of the bishop while he placed something in their mouths. I had heard the Christians pretend to eat the body and drink the blood of their god, and I assumed that this must be the ritual in which they were engaging.

Most bizarrely of all, when a priest went separately to each formation of soldiers, engaging in a chanted dialogue with them, the men knelt down, making the cross sign on their bodies that I had first seen in Britain, and then took up handfuls of earth and put it in their mouths.

"Why are they doing that?" I asked Gretchen, and she replied, "They are showing that God has forgiven their sins and now they are ready for death and burial in the ground if that should be his will for them." I wondered how many of them would, indeed, be dead on the following day.

When the religious ceremonies had been completed there was a great blowing of trumpets and beating of drums, and then one by one the different formations marched off to bivouac overnight close to the battle positions they would occupy on the following day. Gretchen quickly returned to the Duchess, who was now surrounded by Secretary Steinberg, Count Dietrich, the bishop and her leading officers. I was greatly relieved when Sergeant Smet appeared and told me he had found us a billet in a nearby hayshed, where we could spend the night.

Next morning the drums were beating long before daybreak, and fires were lit to give the men warm gruel for breakfast. And then, as the first light of dawn revealed the tips of the eastern hills, the army began moving into position to meet the anticipated approach of the enemy.

The Duchess and her attendants were going to be watching from the squat tower of the small church that stood near the crossroads at the centre of the village. There would be no room for me in their party, but Sergeant Smet had discovered another vantage point. Where the road leading westward crossed the river by a stone bridge, less than a quarter of a mile from the crossroads, there was the ruin of what must once have been a watch-tower guarding the bridge. Now it was juts a pile of moss-covered stones from which small, straggly shrubs protruded through the cracks. But the pile rose up to one corner of the tower that remained intact, at about three times the height of a man, and when we clambered up we found it provided a stable platform on which both of us could stand in comfort.

I had brought with me in my pocket a telescope, the parting gift of my Uncle Kitagawa, which had given me a great deal of pleasure on the voyage from Japan. "You must use this, too," I said, handing it to Smet, "because you'll have a much better idea than I will of what's going on."

He was delighted with the instrument, having never before handled a telescope, and proceeded to tell me as much as he could discover about the army's dispositions. When talking about military matters his Japanese was fluent, but he occasionally stumbled over other, less familiar words and phrases. Earlier in our travels I had learnt from him that his father had been a cloth merchant in Ypres. When the Pasha of the Netherlands had been raising the army that fought the Company at Passchendaele all his father's money had been confiscated as 'taxation', together with all his wagons and horses. With his family reduced to poverty, young Herman had joined the newly-formed second battalion of the Flemish Regiment of Native Infantry a couple of years later, and had steadily worked his way up to the second highest rank open to a native European. In three days' time he would be celebrating his fortieth birthday.

“From what I’ve heard,” he told me, “the man who has been planning the strategy is really Colonel Yamada. He’s the man who trained the Duchess’s Foot Guards. He used to be a Company officer, but I expect he earns a lot more money in Holstein. They say his idea is that Frederick will think the Holstein army will be heading straight for Brunswick city, to stop him getting back into it. So he won’t expect to find them waiting for him here. When the head of his column comes out of the valley into this area of flatter land around the village it will be held by the infantry and the guns drawn up over there.” He pointed almost straight ahead to where, about a quarter of a mile away, I could see through the telescope the backs of three dark masses of men whose flags were catching the first rays of the sun. From their neatly ordered ranks and the absence of any pikes projecting above their heads I could see that the central formation was a battalion of the Foot Guards. And then I noticed that the second battalion of that regiment was drawn up in column much closer to us, presumably acting as a reserve.

“And then,” Smet went on, “the cavalry will smash into them on their right flank. You can see them milling about there, beyond the left flank of the infantry line. I’m sure they’ve had some big arguments about which lot gets to lead the charge. I’d guess that Oldenburg will take that privilege for himself. If Frederick has put his own Guards at the head of the column Oldenburg might get a nasty shock. I hear that the Brandenburg Guards have been trained by a Honanese royal army officer called Colonel Chang. But in all probability it will be some of their old-fashioned cavalry leading the march.

“What will happen after Oldenburg and his bold knights crash into them I wouldn’t want to predict. It’s just primitive stuff with all these fellows in fine armour trying to prove how brave they are. A few well-aimed volleys would get rid of them in no time at all. But the fellows who own big horses think they’re the ones who should be allowed to win the battles – which is why the Company’s army can make short work of them when it needs to. That’s always provided they don’t allow the Honanese to teach them how to use their guns properly.”

There was a series of half-a-dozen loud bangs, and clouds of grey smoke rose up from beyond the serried ranks of the infantry.

"They're off," said Smet. "They must have positioned their field guns in front of the infantry. I expect our man has taught them how to do it and now they've spotted the enemy coming down the valley. I wonder if the Brandenburgers really have been taken by surprise?"

It appeared that they had been, and the battle developed very much as Sergeant Smet had predicted. The cannon discharged a second salvo and then there was a huge crash of musketry, and the resulting cloud of smoke virtually blotted out our vision of the battle line. Soon, however, trumpets screeched out a dozen discordant notes far away on the left flank, and under the soles of our feet we actually felt a tremor as hundreds of horses were launched into a charge nearly half-a-mile away. Through the drifting smoke we caught glimpses of flags and pennons, and the glint of sunshine on steel.

After only a few minutes a tattoo of drumbeats sounded and the masses of infantry began to move slowly away from us. "That charge must have succeeded in smashing their vanguard," said Smet, "but the horsemen will be totally out of control by now. They'll need to get out of the way to let the infantry do their job."

Because there had been no further gunfire we were beginning to have a clearer field of vision when Smet suddenly exclaimed, "There's something happening in the river. Can I have the glass?"

I handed him the telescope and tried to make out what it was that had attracted his attention. "Some of the Brandenburg cavalry are using the river-bed, just along by the bank, to get around the flank; but they're having to do it in single file. I suppose it's too deep farther out into the river," he said, and handed me back the telescope.

I moved the instrument from side to side until suddenly the tiny figure of a horseman appeared in the lens. He had found a place where the bank was lower and was urging his horse up, out of the water. Others were following close behind him, their helmets and cuirasses glinting in the sunshine. "They're wearing Eastern-style uniforms," I said.

"Yes, I think they must be Frederick's Horse Guards," Smet replied. "Their colonel is a bold young fellow called Blücher, I've heard. I expect that's him leading the way."

As a straggling file of horsemen emerged from the riverside and headed eastward towards the road there was a blare of trumpets from one of the reserve formations that was stationed directly in front of our ruined tower, less than a quarter of a mile distant. It was the regiment of Lifeguards, and its leading squadron began moving forward at the trot to intercept the Brandenburgers. The latter, however, were strung out in a long line, the head of which would shortly be clear of the Holsteiners' approaching ranks, while the hindmost riders were starting to veer southward to avoid contact with their enemy.

"They're not trying to make a flank attack," said Smet. "They're just trying to escape from being trapped in the valley."

When the leading fugitives reached the road two field guns positioned in front of the Foot Guards battalion in reserve each fired a round in their direction. As the second projectile exploded I saw two of the horses stumble and crash to the ground."

"Using case shot," said Smet, "Those two were unlucky to be in the wrong place when it burst."

The rest of the Brandenburgers, about two hundred in number, escaped into the distance without injury, and a squadron of Lifeguards was detached in pursuit of them. "They'll probably follow the byroad that leads off to the east," said Smet, "but they'll have a long way to go before they get back to Brandenburg. Maybe they're hoping to link up again with the rest of their army if they escape into the mountains. I'd guess that's where they'll head for – if any of them do escape."

Once again Sergeant Smet was correct in his predictions, although we didn't have confirmation of that until later in the day. He and I abandoned our perch on the ruined tower around mid-morning, when there seemed to be no further prospect of witnessing any action. Back in the village we found the Duchess in a state of great excitement, as messengers arrived telling her the enemy force was in flight, with only a ragged rearguard action covering its retreat.

Standing outside the door of the little church, her cheeks flushed and eyes glowing, she beckoned to a young Lifeguards officer who was part of her escort, giving him an order that sent him racing to his horse and galloping off to the south.

"Did you hear what she said to him?" I asked Smet, who was standing by my side.

"She told him to find Oldenburg and remind him that on no account must he allow Duke Frederick to escape," he said. "They'll be lucky if they catch that wily old Brandenburger."

It was not until early evening, when the Duchess's entourage, to which I had now reattached myself, was sitting down to a rudimentary meal in the village inn, that the young officer returned. He brought with him a report from Oldenburg.

Thanks to a stubborn stand by the Brandenburg Foot Guards near the village of Gross Rhüden, Frederick and the bulk of his cavalry had extricated themselves from the valley, taking a road eastward through the hills. But he had had to abandon his guns (including those he had captured from Joseph), and the remnants of his infantry had nearly all been taken prisoner. And the best news was that, with his horses exhausted, Frederick had taken refuge in the ancient walled town of Goslar, where even now Oldenburg was making certain that he was totally surrounded, with no possibility of escape.

Gretchen, with whom I was sharing a makeshift table on an upended barrel, translated for me what was being said, and added the comment that, although the walls of Goslar were very old, they were also very thick. "But with all the guns that he has now I'm sure it won't take the Count long to make a hole in them," she went on, her eyes sparkling with excitement. "We'll carry Duke Frederick back to Hamburg in a cart before the week is out."

CHAPTER 9

The siege of Goslar was four days old when the first news arrived of an army approaching from the west. Oldenburg had set up his headquarters to direct the siege in the hamlet of Oker, about a mile from the ancient walls, and I had accompanied the Duchess's entourage to join him there. Operations were delayed because on the first day a heavy downpour made the roads muddy and the Holsteiners' four heaviest guns, being drawn by teams of oxen, got bogged down. And then, on the third day, when they had finally been put in position, a troop of Brandenburg cavalry sallied out after dusk and succeeded in spiking two of them. But now, Oldenburg assured the Duchess, the bombardment was about to begin. So she left the town of Vienenburg, where she had been lodging, and arrived at his headquarters in the village inn just after midday.

Then the bearer of momentous news arrived, a young man who that morning had ridden all the way from Hildesheim and still looked full of energy, though his horse was exhausted. I learned later that his name was Scharnhorst, and although he was the son of a wealthy peasant he had gained rapid promotion in the bodyguard of the late Duke of Brunswick because of his courage and sagacity. He brought news to the Duchess that a large force of the Company's troops had arrived at Hildesheim the night before and was even now on its way to Goslar.

I was standing with some twenty others in the crowded room when Scharnhorst delivered his news, and the Duchess turned instantly to me, asking, "What does this mean? Why has the Company sent an army into Brunswick?"

Taken aback at first, I stammered, "I… I really don't know, Your Grace." Then, recovering my wits, I added, "But I know that the Governor-General was very concerned that you shouldn't be the loser in these conflicts. I expect he heard about Duke Frederick's early victories and sent the army to support you, if you should need it."

"Well, I don't need it," she replied. "But you're probably right. In his last message to me your master, Okada, said he was looking forward to greeting me as the Duchess Regent of Brunswick. I am just surprised he didn't tell me that an army was on its way in case I needed help. And help usually has a price attached to it. However, I expect we shall soon find out. Do you think Okada is with the army?"

"I'm afraid he didn't tell me his plans, Your Grace. My orders were to return to Antwerp when you had been successful; or if things went wrong for you to go as quickly as possible to General Kuroki, who would be just over the frontier, at Enschede."

"Then I am sure Okada will have come with General Kuroki," said the Duchess.

Okada had, indeed, accompanied the army, but so had the Governor-General himself, and it was from him that a message arrived at the Holstein headquarters next morning. Conveyed by a smartly-uniformed captain of the Walloon Native Infantry, it requested an early meeting with the Duchess. She decided to go to the Company's encampment and her coach was rapidly prepared. I was one of a small group allowed to follow behind, which I did, uncomfortably, on a borrowed horse. Oldenburg himself rode ahead of the coach. And behind us we heard the first reverberations of cannon fire as the bombardment of Goslar recommenced in the morning light.

As soon as the picquets sighted our approach to the Company's army, camped near the village of Hahndorf, General Kuroki came riding out to greet us. He first exchanged pleasantries with Oldenburg – doubtless congratulating him on his victory – and then dismounted to greet the Duchess in her coach. We continued our journey on the road, with troop formations on either side, and I noticed that, although the men were at ease with muskets stacked, they were occupying defensive positions, with batteries of cannon in place ahead of the infantry. On our left I recognized a battalion of the Flanders Native Infantry and on our right an imperial battalion which, from the light blue facings on their scarlet coats, I could see was the Shizuoka Regiment.

When we arrived in the village of Hahndorf Governor-General Higashi emerged from the village inn to greet us, and then escorted the Duchess and Oldenburg inside the building. The rest of us were not invited. I dismounted from my unfriendly horse and gave it to a trooper in the Duchess's escort to hold.

The village street was busy with Company officers moving to and from the headquarters, which apparently comprised not only the inn but also a couple of tents pitched alongside it. To exercise my legs I began walking back along the street and immediately a voice called out, "Hashimoto! What are you doing here?" I turned to see Takahashi Nayata, my friend on the long voyage, dressed in the scarlet coat and black trousers of the native infantry, and wearing a sword by his side.

"I've been keeping an eye on the Duchess of Holstein for my boss, Okada," I replied. "I thought your battalion might be here; but do you know why the Governor-General has brought up the army? The war is nearly over. The Holsteiners have got Duke Frederick trapped in that town up there, and it won't be long before they've made a breach in the walls."

"I don't know what Higashi's up to," he replied. "We've been told we're in friendly territory but we've got to stay on guard because the situation could change at any time. So the guns are loaded."

I asked how he was enjoying life in the army and his reply was enthusiastic. Most of his fellow-officers had been welcoming, and he was beginning to get to know the men in his platoon, and to understand their language. And he had not, so far, been involved in any violent activities.

He asked about my experiences and I described the trip to Britain and also my earlier visit to Hamburg, but I refrained from mentioning my more intimate contacts with the Duchess. Needless to say, Takahashi wanted to know more about Ermyntrude, and teased me when I admitted that I hadn't yet made any attempt to seduce her. "You never know: you might end up one day producing somebody like that," he said, pointing to a horseman who had just ridden into the street.

The newcomer was an impressive figure, mounted on a powerful black horse and wearing a yellow uniform coat with silver lacing and a Western-style helmet with a tall, red-over-white plume. His nose was long and pointed but the rest of his features looked East Asian. I gazed at him in bewilderment.

"That's Colonel Shunzo," said Takahashi. "He has his own regiment of irregular cavalry, called Shunzo's Horse. His father came from Kyushu and married the daughter of a native aristocrat, Count

Egmont, and the Colonel was one of the results. When he grew up he followed the Muslim practice and he now has six wives and I don't know how many children – the makings of another regiment, I expect. Has this British girl got a long nose?"

"She has a very pretty nose," I replied, "but I have no reason to think she would want to get married to me."

"Who said anything about getting married?" he retorted. "It's time you started having some fun."

"Are there many AisEuropeans in the army?" I asked.

"Quite a few. I think a lot of them are in the artillery. I suppose it's because most of them get a good education in the Company school."

We talked for a few minutes more about places where Takahashi had been, including uneventful patrols on the frontier with the Pashalik of Lorraine, and then he had to hurry back to his adjutant, from whom he had been taking a report to headquarters. When he had gone I strolled back to the inn and waited outside.

Eventually the door opened and the sentries on either side of it sprang to attention as the Duchess emerged, accompanied by the Governor-General. Behind them walked Oldenburg, with a facial expression like clouds before a thunderstorm; and behind him came Okada, who gave me an almost imperceptible nod when his watchful eye caught sight of me.

Higashi exchanged a few words with the Duchess before assisting her into her carriage, by which time Oldenburg had already mounted his horse and the Holstein party was ready to move off. I went quickly to my horse, taking its reins from the trooper who was holding them, but Okada signalled to me to remain where I was. As the Duchess's carriage got under way with much creaking and straining he came across to me, saying, "We shall be following in a few moments. You will accompany me. I hope you have your writing-pad with you." Fortunately the pad was in the pocket of my coat.

When the horses had been brought round to the front of the inn the Governor-General mounted and rode off, accompanied by his secretary, Masaki. Okada and I followed behind, and after us rode a detachment of the South Hokkaido Light Horse. As we rode Okada began to tell me what had been happening.

"The Governor-General has decided to play the part of peacemaker," he said. "We are going to have a talk with Duke Frederick and make him an offer he will be unable to refuse."

"But isn't he already beaten?" I asked. "In a matter of days – maybe hours – the Holsteiners will have blasted a breach in the city wall, and with no infantry he won't be able to resist an assault for very long."

"Quite right," said Okada. "That's why he's not going to refuse the Governor-General's offer. If he agrees to recognize Sophia's son, Otto, as the rightful Duke of Brunswick, and signs treaties of friendship and alliance against third-party aggression with her and with the Company, then the Company's army will provide him and his remaining troops with safe conduct back across his own frontier to the city of Magdeburg. Oh, and there is one other thing – the Company will hospitably arrange for his Honanese advisers, if they have survived the battle, to be provided with berths on the first West Europaman sailing from Antwerp."

"Has the Duchess really agreed to this?" I asked. "I thought her plan was to capture Frederick and take over Brandenburg herself."

"Once again you are absolutely right." Okada turned in his saddle and gave me one of his rare smiles. "The message that you sent me by Kees Zalm was extremely helpful in confirming that suspicion. It might have been difficult to persuade her and her victorious general that that was not a good idea had we not brought these fine fellows along with us." He gestured towards the troop formations through which we were now passing.

"Not that they were mentioned in the discussion, of course," he went on. "The Governor-General pointed out that the prolongation of hostilities might lead to others getting involved. Joseph and Albrecht, for example, still have substantial forces available if they should decide to make a second attempt. But the Company would be willing to guarantee the new status quo, which would give the Duchess Sophia everything she has publicly said she wants. And the Duchess must be well aware that there is a limit to how long she can keep her army in the field. These little duchies may look very impressive when they put all their petty landowners on to horses, waving swords and lances, but to keep them there they have to squeeze the resources of their miserable peasants, who have very little to be squeezed. I wouldn't mind betting that Her Grace's army is already beginning to run short of supplies. No doubt they were looking forward to getting their hands on some plunder in Brandenburg, but that would hardly have been an auspicious start for the Duchess as a new ruler.

"Oldenburg isn't happy; but at least he can celebrate victory with remarkably few casualties. If he'd had to storm a breach here with the Brandenburgers defending it he would have lost a lot more – though I suppose that might not matter to him. I don't know how these European warlords think."

"Do you think Duke Frederick will accept the Governor-General's offer?" I asked.

"I think he'll be very grateful for it," Okada replied. "From what I've heard he's a shrewd old boy and he'll recognize that it offers him his only hope of survival."

As usual, Okada was right. We met the famous old warrior in the Rathaus of Goslar, an ancient and once beautiful building that showed signs of neglect and decay. The same description might well have been applied to the Duke, with his sunken cheeks and prominent eyes, and grey hair secured in a long pigtail that hung well below his rounded shoulders. He greeted us with dignified courtesy, speaking in fluent Latin and even jesting with the Governor-General as soon as it became apparent that what he was being offered was an avenue of escape. In less than two hours the important documents had all been signed, with Rendsburg, the Duchess's High Chamberlain, representing the Holsteiners.

In the late afternoon the Brandenburg troops departed through the east gate of the city on their way to Magdeburg. They were escorted by the South Hokkaido Light Horse and Shunzo's Horse, and their efforts to appear undaunted were hampered by having been obliged to leave behind much of their equipment and personal accoutrements to compensate the citizens for the food and drink they had seized during their stay. From the gate-tower Okada and I watched the long, dispirited procession of mounted men, followed by carts containing the less seriously wounded, wend its way downhill and into the distance.

"Going to war is like playing at dice," said Okada. "A week ago Frederick must have thought his victory was secure. But now we have to get our army home again without allowing it to do any damage on the way. Tomorrow we're going to Brunswick city to lend our weight to the inauguration of young Otto as their new Duke – and Sophia as his Regent, of course. Apparently she's been keeping him a day's march behind the army, out of harm's way."

It was actually on the day after next that the ceremony took place in Brunswick, for the journey had left everyone weary and covered in grime. As Okada remarked, "On state occasions appearances are much more important than the words that are spoken since, anyhow, very few people can hear the words."

Otto's styles and titles were proclaimed in the city square as he stood beside an ancient bronze figure of a lion. The bronze lion, I was told by Gretchen (beside whom I was able to stand during the ceremony), was six hundred years old and commemorated a very famous ancient Duke of Saxony called Henry the Lion who lived at the time, and who had built the city's biggest Christian temple, called the Dom.

When this outdoor event was concluded all the important people walked in procession to the Dom for a religious ceremony. Since Gretchen had to attend on the Duchess I followed on my own, and stood at the back of the big stone building. Its massive pillars and round-headed arches looked as if they had been constructed by giants in some legendary, bygone era. Without Gretchen's help I could understand little of what was happening, even though the language being used was Latin. The air was filled with the sweet, sickly smell of incense and the mournful chanting of the monks reminded me of the day I visited the temple in Britain – the day before I met Ermyntrude. Suddenly I realized how much I missed her, how much I wanted to tell her about all the events of the past four weeks (omitting the intimate encounters with Sophia) and how much I wanted to see again the responsive sparkle in her bright blue eyes as we sat face to face in the privacy of Count Furaya's library.

I was aroused from my reverie by a great shout of "Vivat", repeated three times, by the whole congregation, and soon after that the ceremony came to an end. Then there was a celebratory feast (of sorts, for it had clearly been put together very hurriedly) in the city hall, which Gretchen told me was five hundred years old. By the time the feast was over I was ready to look for a quiet spot in which to have a nap, but Okada bore down on me saying, "The Governor-General and I are going to meet a very interesting character. You can come along with us." It was an invitation I could not refuse.

As we walked along the narrow street of tall, half-timbered houses, following in the wake of the Duchess and her secretary, Steinberg, with whom Governor-General Higashi was deep in conversation, Okada told me who it was we were going to meet. "He came here with Frederick two months ago but because he's very old – well over eighty, they say – he didn't accompany the army when it marched off to do battle. For a good many years he has been one of Frederick's closest advisers, but it seems he is also respected by educated people all over northern Europa because he has written a number of books about government and history – and also some poetry in his youth. That's why the Governor-General wants to meet him. As you know, he's always eager to find out more about European culture."

"Is this man a Brandenburger?" I asked.

"No. He actually comes from the Pashalik of Champagne, on our southern border, where the language they speak is called 'French'. At one time he was a kind of senior priest, called a 'canon', in the capital city of Reims. That was the time when he wrote most of his poetry."

"A priest writing poetry – that sounds strange," I said.

"You have to remember," said Okada, "that in this part of the world the only way in which a young man can get any education – unless his parents are wealthy – is by becoming a priest or a monk. I would guess that's why Canon Arouet entered the priesthood. It's not for his piety that he's famous. I believe that some of his earlier poems were about relationships with women, which is why all his poetry was written under an assumed name. I've heard the name but I can't remember what it was."

"But how did he get to Brandenburg?" I asked.

"The story I've heard is that he spoke up for some Muslim peasants in Champagne who were going to be horribly punished by the pasha for not paying their taxes. Most of the people there, apart from the ruling class and the warriors, are Christians, but there are also some descendants of Muslim soldiers who were given farms when they retired from the army. According to the story, in one village they thought they should be let off paying tax because they were of the same religion as the pasha – and they'd had a bad harvest. The pasha was having none of it. He was afraid their defiance of his tax-collector would set a bad example; so he sentenced them to be impaled."

"Impaled?" I queried, never having heard of that punishment.

"It's a punishment the Turks usually reserve for people who have given them a lot of trouble. A sharpened stake is inserted in the victim's anus and pushed up through his body to exit through his mouth. The trick is to ensure that it doesn't kill him on the way, so that for as long as possible he can be displayed alive to other potential offenders, who may take warning from the sufferer's fate. Apparently a skilful executioner will be able to achieve that grisly result."

I shuddered at the image his words had conjured up and asked, "How did the priest get involved?"

"When he heard what was happening - possibly because he knew the village where the victims came from – he went to the pasha's palace and pleaded with him not to be so cruel. But the pasha wasn't impressed and threw him into prison, with the threat that he might share the peasants' fate for daring to object."

"How did he escape?"

"According to the story, which is virtually a legend by now, a Muslim gaoler was so impressed by Arouet having pleaded on behalf of his co-religionists that he let him out through a window; and afterwards he told the story that he'd seen the prisoner carried up into the sky by an angel. There happened to be a convenient thunderstorm that night. Needless to say, a lot of people still choose to believe the angel story, which was greatly reinforced when, a few weeks later, the pasha had a stroke and lost the ability to walk or speak."

"That's incredible," I said, "but why did Canon Arouet go to Brandenburg?"

"It seems that he escaped down the river in a boat to Normandy, which by that time had broken away from the Empire under a Christian duke. But the duke was anxious to avoid a conflict with his neighbour, the pasha, and so he put Arouet on a ship that was sailing to Hamburg. Frederick heard about his arrival there and invited him to Brandenburg. He had been very impressed by a long poem Arouet had written about how a Christian ruler ought to behave, and so he wanted to meet him. And Arouet has remained at his court ever since – nearly thirty years, I think."

I was now eagerly looking forward to meeting this legendary figure, and when we were ushered into his lodging I was at first disappointed to see a small, wizened, sharp-featured man in a stained black cassock and a black skullcap, who greeted us with an air of weary resignation. The Duchess opened the conversation by complimenting him lavishly on his reputation as a writer and a defender of justice. And she went on to reassure him that, as soon as he was ready to travel, she would place at his disposal a comfortable coach to take him back to his home in Potsdam.

Arouet's face brightened at this reassurance and he said, "I shall want to hasten back to my generous host, Duke Frederick, at this time of disappointment for him, and give him what comfort I can. But I shall be careful to refrain from reminding him that I was not among those who encouraged him to come to Brunswick. I recall that, when his Archbishop assured him it was the will of God that his beneficent rule should be extended across the whole of northern Germany, I warned him that from my reading of history it appeared that God was always on the side of the big battalions."

The Governor-General laughed and said, "I think you gave him very good advice. May I ask whether, in your opinion, Duke Frederick attaches a lot of importance to ascertaining what the will of his god might be before he decides what to do?"

Arouet paused for a few moments with eyes half closed, stroking his chin with his left hand. Then he said, "His Grace is not a superstitious man, unlike some of those around him; but although he can command obedience he knows well how important it is to arouse the enthusiasm of his subjects for policies that might be doubtful or even dangerous. Adding a divine dimension to his reasons for adopting them can be very useful.

"In the more mundane matters of government," he went on, "His Grace is also a generous supporter of the Church. He is well aware that for the majority of his people life has little more to offer than toil and hardship, sickness and the ever-present certainty of death. The Church sustains them with the promise of happier times in a world beyond the grave. And also because, with little opportunity for education, they lack the capacity to understand the philosophical arguments that underpin the maintenance of law and order in a civilized society, the threat of divine retribution for wrongdoers and rebels is a potent reinforcement to the authority of a ruler. I sometimes think that if God did not exist it would be necessary to invent him.

"However, invoking the divine will is not without dangers and disadvantages, as I am sure Your Grace is well aware," he went on, with an inclination of his head in the direction of the Duchess. "Those whose profession it is to act as intermediaries between earth and heaven can lay claim to being its interpreters, and on occasion their interpretations can be singularly inconvenient. I have observed that they often lay stress on those aspects of God's purposes which most closely accord with their own immediate interests. Every powerful preacher to whom I have listened has painted a picture in my mind of a God who closely resembles himself. If God did indeed make us all in his image, we have certainly returned the compliment."

The Duchess smiled, and asked him, "What does Duke Frederick think of the proposal that we Germans should try to restore the old Holy Roman Empire?"

"I believe, Your Grace, he shares my view of that historical agglomeration: it was neither holy, nor Roman, nor in any way an empire. All our ancient history, as one of our wits once remarked, is no more than accepted fiction."

"But may I ask you a question, Your Excellency?" he continued, turning to Higashi, who nodded his head in acknowledgement. "I have heard much about this 'Tsunami of Reason' which has flowed through the minds of educated people in East Asia and is changing the ways in which they see the world. Will this new understanding enable those who have it to make changes to the physical world in ways that hitherto have not been possible?"

"It is already doing so," Higashi replied. "A hundred small discoveries are constantly opening the way to ever greater advances.

Medical men, for example, have discovered how to stop the spread of smallpox, a disease that I know takes a heavy toll in this continent; and so the lives of many people will be changed. And almost every year, it seems, some new machine is devised to undertake a task that until now could be accomplished only by the strength and skills of humans or of animals. New ways of making iron are multiplying the quantity and quality of that material so that now it is available for many purposes. I think that our children's children will live in a world that will be very different from ours – in East Asia, but maybe also in Europa."

Arouet nodded his head three times, very slowly. "A world in which men can feel themselves to be the masters of Nature, not its slaves – I wonder how that will change the ways in which they treat each other. If they stop believing in absurdities will they cease to perpetrate atrocities; or will they in the name of reason fabricate new absurdities to guide their actions, and go on persecuting one another? As the end of my life draws nearer it makes me sad to reflect that history is just a tableau of crimes and misfortunes. Do you think it possible that one day this 'Tsunami of Reason' may come flooding into Europa?"

"Even in East Asia its influence is only just beginning to be felt," Higashi replied. "A new way of making iron can be perfected in a decade, but a new way of understanding the world takes generations to be accepted. Nevertheless, along with the silk and the tea, the ceramics and the cotton, I am sure that the Company is bringing new ideas into this sub-continent, and one day the present trickle may become a flood. And I am sure that the minds of your people will be as capable of exercising the power of reason as those of any other race. If I may say so without offence, you are in your own person the living proof of that assurance."

Arouet's eyes lit up and his sunken lips twitched into a smile as he savoured the compliment. "You do me too much honour," he said, "but I hope that what you predict will one day come true. Europa needs to break free from its history, and maybe only a force from beyond its shores can sweep away its barriers and divisions, and give its people the vision of a different way to live. But, as you say, that kind of change takes generations to accomplish, and the natural impatience men are prone to will make its accomplishment all the slower. They will see a vision of perfection and will rage destructively against the smallness of those improvements by which they move towards it. The best is the enemy of the good."

Glancing at a quill pen and ink pot on the table beside his chair, the Duchess asked, "Are you writing another book? Do you never cease from working?"

"Indeed not, Your Grace," he replied. "In a long lifetime I have observed that work banishes those three great evils, boredom, vice and poverty."

"And this time what will your pen produce for our delight?" she asked. "Will it be history, or statecraft or poetry?"

"You have heard my opinion of history; and the observations on statecraft that I have written in the past have often been applauded but very seldom have they been applied. So on this occasion my efforts are being devoted to the composition of a poem. Before you ask" – he raised his right hand in an admonitory gesture - "I shall tell you that its subject is the wanderings through many lands of a young man – a young man not unlike the one who waits upon Your Excellencies." Smiling, he nodded in my direction and I felt, for some unaccountable reason, that I had been accorded an honour.

Arouet continued, "In the course of his travels he meets with many misfortunes and witnesses much cruelty. He observes in the people he encounters a great deal of irrational behaviour; but his own good sense and courage enable him to survive. And you might suppose that, having overcome so many perils, he is then permitted to lead the most pleasing life imaginable, but that is not the outcome. Happy endings are for fairy tales and hagiographers. He ends his life as I am ending mine, finding in his work the meaning of his existence, and not entertaining false hopes of receiving some reward in a paradise beyond the grave."

"Under which of your names will you publish the poem?" asked Okada, who had not previously spoken.

"Among the few who are able to read I think there are not many who will be unaware of my opinions," he replied. "Nevertheless, I choose not to give gratuitous offence to those who are scandalized by any overt association of a man of the cloth with a view of the human condition that is not sanctified by Holy Scripture. So the poem has been written by Voltaire."

His toothless mouth opened wide in a yawn and he closed his eyes. It was evident that our audience was at an end.

CHAPTER 10

Fresh horses made the journey from Brunswick to Hamburg a swift one for the Governor-General's entourage. I was fortunate enough to be attached to it, for the army's march back to the Netherlands, taking care to avoid upsetting the natives on the way, was much slower. In Hamburg we boarded the Imperial Navy sloop *Usugumo*, and in less than two days we were entering the estuary of the Scheldt.

As I stood on the deck watching Walcheren Island glide past in the distance I suddenly became aware for the first time of just how momentous had been the events to which I had been a witness. Within the space of two months a sizeable territory had twice changed its ruler; and the Company had demonstrated unmistakably its power to shape the outcome of events in northern Europa. And although my role had been a fairly insignificant one, I had been not just a spectator but an actor in these happenings that would one day be recorded in the history books.

I experienced an urgent need to tell somebody about what I had seen and what I had done – somebody who was interested not just in the events but also in me. Had I now been on my way home to Japan I would have been thinking of what I would say to my father and my brother. (My mother, whose horizons sadly did not extend beyond her neighbours' gardens, would not have been interested.) But even if I were now to write a letter it would be months before they read it. There was one person who might, just, want to hear what I had to say. And when I thought about Ermyntrude the memory returned to me of how much I had wanted, back in Brunswick, to tell her what I had seen and heard. Now it became part of an overwhelming desire to be with her again, to hear her voice, to make her laugh – and to see in her eyes that she wanted to be with me.

When we finally disembarked the light was beginning to fade and there was no time left for paying calls. Next morning I woke late from a deep slumber and had to go without breakfast in order to present myself for work on time. When I arrived Okada was already immersed in a stack of reports that had arrived in his absence. We worked steadily through the day, taking only half-an-hour to eat a dish of rice and codfish, followed by a handful of the delicious local fruit called 'strawberries', which were then in season. However, by the late afternoon even Okada's appetite for work had begun to slacken and he told me that I could go, adding, "No doubt you will have things to sort out after your long absence."

When I had washed off the sweat of the day and changed my clothes I hurried through the winding streets to Count Furaya's house. The door was answered by the same liveried manservant I had seen on my first visit, and I told him I had come to see Ermyntrude.

"Mistress Ermyntrude has gone out," he said.

"Where has she gone? Do you know when she will be back?"

"I understand that she is at the Steen with Lieutenant Hirose," he replied. "She said only that she would return before curfew."

For a moment I stared at him in astonishment. It had never occurred to me that Ermyntrude might not be at home when I called on her. And then I recovered my wits, telling myself that, after all, she hadn't known that I was going to visit at that particular time.

"Will you tell her that I called, please, and that I hope to call again tomorrow evening?" I said. "And give her these." I handed him a punnet of strawberries I had bought from a large, pink-cheeked woman in a white bonnet on my way through the Grote Markt.

As I turned away from the door all the sense of hope and elation that had propelled my steps towards it seemed to drain out of me. Ermyntrude had gone to Hirose. No doubt he had seen his opportunity to move in when I was away. He was taller and handsomer than me, and five or six years older, with that much more experience of the world, and of women. And weren't sailors notorious for their attractiveness to innocent girls, and for the carelessness with which they abandoned their lovers in one port when they sailed away to the next? At this very moment Hirose might be enjoying the delights of my lovely Ermyntrude's body without caring a jot for the brilliance of her mind or the sweetness of her nature. Why had I been so slow to tell her how much she meant to me? Had I left it too late to win her affections for myself? Those were the thoughts that jostled in my mind as I trudged despondently back along Wolstraat.

Jealousy was an emotion that I had never previously experienced to any great degree, possibly because I had never before felt so strongly about any woman as I now, to my surprise, discovered that I felt about Ermyntrude. Somehow I had assumed that she would just be waiting for me if I should ever want to make our relationship more intimate. I had given no thought to what she might be feeling or wanting. And now it was too late.

The Regulatory Council met the following morning to hear the Governor-General's report on the events in Brunswick, and I took my place with the other secretaries as before. The only change from the previous meeting was that Lord Justice Oku had recovered from his illness and was sitting alongside the four Councillors at the far side of the long table. When the Minutes had been read Governor-General Higashi quickly launched into his report, describing the events that led up to his confrontation with the Duchess.

"Although Duchess Sophia has been a reliable ally, and we favoured her bid to take possession of Brunswick," he said, "we had also become aware that she had grandiose ambitions to make herself the mistress of the whole of Germany. Her first step towards achieving them would have been to capture Duke Frederick and add Brandenburg to the conquest of Brunswick. Whether or not she could ever have succeeded in welding that rabble of feudal warlords into an effective state is questionable, but it was a risk I did not feel we were justified in taking. A large, unified and inherently warlike state on our north-eastern frontier could very quickly have become a threat to the Company's security.

"Fortunately General Kuroki was able to move the army with admirable speed" – he inclined his head towards the general in salutation – "so that we arrived at Goslar before the Holsteiners were able to complete their assault on its walls. I was therefore able to assume the role of mediator, seeking to end the conflict without further bloodshed. Without the presence of General Kuroki's battalions I doubt whether my words would have been listened to, but once it became clear that we were not going to permit an assault to be made on Goslar Sophia, who I think is a pragmatist, was content to settle for the gains she had already made.

"Frederick, when we went to see him inside the beleaguered city, was mightily relieved, for he knew he had no hope of surviving the siege. He was also very surprised that we were offering him a chance to recover his position. As you know, he was being subsidized by the

Honanese, who were helping him to Easternize his army – insofar as it would allow itself to be Easternized. He must have known that their intention was to use him as an ally against us, and in that role he could have been very effective once he had taken possession of Brunswick.

"In the circumstances, he was very happy to swap our friendship for theirs. His little gang of Honanese officers and advisers became my 'guests', and they left for Asia on this morning's tide – Admiral Katsura kindly made the arrangements. So now, although the Duchess Sophia may be feeling frustrated, she has doubled the size of her dominions; and she must be well aware that when she turns her face towards us in the west she also turns her back to our new friend, Duke Frederick, in the east."

"That would appear to be a very satisfactory outcome, Your Excellency," said Count Furaya, "not least because it brought a swift conclusion to the slaughter and destruction."

"And also because it didn't end up with the Company taking responsibility for yet more troublesome territory," said Councillor Hiraoka. "I trust we can now get on with opening up Brandenburg to exports."

"You will be pleased to know that we included a clause about that in the Goslar Agreement," Higashi replied. "Our fish will very soon be finding its way there through Hamburg, and the woollens that the Honanese were selling them from La Rochelle will shortly be replaced by our superior products from here in Flanders."

"What about the trade in tea and spices?" asked Councillor Akiyama. "I believe the Honanese had built up a very brisk business through Frankfurt on the Oder."

"That is correct," said Higashi, "and from the end of this year those two monopolies will be transferred to the Company. I am sure Mr Matsuzaki will take the earliest opportunity to inform Edo of the likely growth in demand. It would be unfortunate if the next convoy didn't bring a sufficient increase of supplies to cope with it."

"Of course, Your Excellency," said Matsuzaki, the Senior Factor responsible for Commerce, leaning over the table and inclining his head towards the Governor-General with every indication of enthusiasm. "I shall be greatly obliged if Admiral Katsura will ask the squadron commander to let me know when the next fast vessel is due to sail for Japan."

“That’s all very satisfactory, Your Excellency,” said Hiraoka, “but I trust the Company hasn’t been committed to assist Duke Frederick if he should find himself in trouble with any of his neighbours in the future. Were there any military clauses in the Goslar Agreement?”

“Our only promise to Duke Frederick was to fill, to a limited extent, the gap left by the departure of the Honanese. I have undertaken to recruit on his behalf a number of experienced officers to help him reorganize his army,” Higashi replied. “It will be greatly to our advantage to have some reliable people of our own choosing keeping an eye on things in Berlin.”

While the Governor-General was speaking one of his clerks entered the room and tiptoed across to his Secretary, Masaki, handing him a sealed packet. Masaki looked at the inscription on it and instantly took it to the table, placing it in front of Higashi. “Something for me marked ‘Extremely urgent’,” said the Governor-General. “Where has it come from?”

The clerk, who was still standing behind him, replied, “The frigate *Akebono* has just docked, Your Excellency. The captain himself brought the packet for you. He’s waiting outside.”

“Ask him to come in, and bring him a seat at the table. You will excuse me, gentlemen, while I look at the contents. This appears to be a communication from the Imperial Chancellor himself.”

Everyone within sight of Higashi’s face seemed to be watching it intently for any indication of the kind of news contained in the message he was reading. They glanced away only momentarily when the officer in a weather-stained naval uniform entered the room and was given a seat at the corner of the table, near to General Kuroki.

There were several pages to be scanned, but eventually Higashi looked up from the letter and addressed himself to the newcomer. “Captain Kimura, you are to be congratulated on the speed with which you have managed to bring us this vitally important news. I am sure that its swift arrival will make a vital contribution to the success of operations in the coming weeks. We shall do our utmost to make full use of the advantages which its early arrival confers upon us.

“Gentlemen,” he said, turning his head to look at the four Councillors sitting directly across the table from him, “Japan is at war with Honan, Shantung and Fukien. Those three unlikely allies have got together to exploit in their own interests the difficulties which, it appears, our government is having in suppressing the rebellion of the New Continent colonists. Consequently we are here” – he tapped the letter on the table in front of him with his forefinger – “charged by His Imperial Majesty to promote with all vigour hostilities against his enemies in this hemisphere. We can be sure that before many weeks have passed our Honanese and Shantungese neighbours will be receiving similar instructions from their governments. But thanks to Captain Kimura’s superb seamanship I think we may have a small advantage of surprise, and we must make the most of it.”

Although the news had not been totally unexpected because of the recent rumours of impending conflict that had been circulating with the new arrival of every vessel from East Asia, there was nevertheless an interval of stunned silence following the Governor-General’s announcement. Then Councillor Hiraoka solemnly shook his head and said, “Yet another distraction from the business of doing business; but I fear that on this occasion we have no choice.”

“If we can gain the upper hand at La Rochelle and in Britain before the Honanese manage to get a fleet round here we should be doing a lot more business before very long,” said Baron Nagata.

“Exactly so. And that must be our priority from this moment onward,” said Higashi. “We don’t know how long it will be before our enemies receive news of what has happened and we must make the most of our advantage. General Kuroki, Admiral Katsura, I am sure you would agree.”

“Absolutely, Your Excellency,” Kuroki replied. “We haven’t a moment to lose.”

“I have a fast schooner that can take your orders to Bordeaux before nightfall,” added Katsura.

“Yes, we have got to seize La Rochelle before the Honanese can begin to fortify it,” said Higashi. “It’s a very strong defensive position.” (I had read somewhere that in the treaty ending the ‘Six Years War’, some fourteen years earlier, La Rochelle had been returned by us to the Honanese, but on condition that its fortifications were not rebuilt.)

“The Bordeaux Army should have no trouble taking it over,” said Kuroki, “but we can be sure that the so-called Sultan of Aquitaine will move against us the moment he knows the game’s afoot. The Honanese have been subsidizing him for many years, and our Bordeaux Army isn’t strong enough to defeat him. In a month or two he could probably put forty thousand men into the field. We shall need to send a strong corps down there without delay.”

“This is the moment when we have to put our own alliances to the test,” said Higashi. “As General Kuroki rightly says, an army must be sent to Guyenne, to see off the Sultan of Aquitaine. We can call on the Duke of Normandy to give it safe passage through his territory and then, if need be, it will have to fight its way across the Pashalik of Anjou to La Rochelle. But I think it unlikely that the Pasha will put up any serious resistance, especially if he’s taken by surprise. And at the same time we can call on the Emir of Touraine to join in our attack on the Sultan. He’s been waiting to get his revenge ever since the Sultan stole Limousin from him. The important thing is that we prevent the Honanese from establishing a foothold down there. I’m sure at this moment they’re preparing a fleet to attack us, if it’s not already on its way.”

“We’ll be ready for them,” said Admiral Katsura, “but all the same I hope that Edo is sending us a few more ships of the line. If we have to undertake amphibious operations the fleet will be stretched to its limit.”

“You will be pleased to know,” said Higashi, looking down at the letter on the table, “the Chancellor informs me that Rear-Admiral Shimanura is preparing to sail immediately with a squadron of three seventy-fours and a fifty to reinforce you. And you will indeed be required to undertake amphibious operations. If we are to be secure in this conflict we must remove the threat of intervention from the Shantungese in Britain. Their small squadron could be a nuisance, but more importantly they could provide a base for the Honanese fleet when it arrives. We have to take control of that island, and quickly.”

Councillor Hiraoka threw up his hands despairingly and exclaimed, “More territory! How is Your Excellency going to govern it, and what will be the cost?”

Ignoring the interruption, Admiral Katsura said, “Your Excellency is absolutely right. Control of Britain is the key to sending those Honanese scoundrels home for the very last time – the ones we don't send to the bottom of the sea, that is. And it is my pleasure to inform you that we have just completed an operational plan to destroy the Shantungese squadron and seize the port of London – if General Kuroki can provide the necessary invasion force. If we can take their squadron by surprise in its anchorage in the Medway river we can send in a flotilla of fireships and burn them to a crisp. And after that we can sail upstream and bombard their fortress at London till they realize that a speedy surrender will be in their own best interests. No doubt Your Excellency will be able to provide the officer in command with the surrender terms that can be offered to the Shantungese Governor."

"Yes, indeed. And are you really ready to move immediately?"

"We are, Your Excellency. Only yesterday Commodore Wada completed a plan of operations for me. He had the help of Lieutenant Hirose, whose visit to Britain three months ago provided us with the exact information that we needed to formulate a strategy. I shall be promoting that young man very shortly. And Count Furaya may be interested to know that the young British woman he brought back with him gave us some valuable assistance with the geographical details, and the barbarous names of the places with which we shall have to familiarize ourselves. The Count was kind enough to lend us her services for the whole day yesterday which, very fortunately, enabled us to get the plan on to paper. It's ready now for distribution to those officers who will be needing it."

His words exploded in my mind like a firecracker. Ermyntrude had not been spending yesterday in some kind of dalliance with Lieutenant Hirose: she had been helping the navy to plan its invasion of Britain. I might still be in with a chance to… I wasn't quite sure exactly what I wanted to do, but I knew that I wanted to see those strange blue, European eyes smiling at me again. For a few minutes my thoughts were all in Count Furaya's library and I scarcely heard what was being said at the table.

They were discussing the arrangements for a surprise attack that would cripple the Shantungese naval squadron and capture the city of London, and for a simultaneous attack on the southern British port of Southampton, which Admiral Katsura said could also be used as a base by the Honanese when their expected fleet arrived in European waters. I heard Katsura ask, "Is Your Excellency prepared to take nominal possession of the whole island in the name of the Crown, once we've captured London – and, if we're lucky the Governor along with it? If we don't take a firm grip on the civil power straight away I fear that some of the natives might take the opportunity to stir up trouble, and the Honanese would be delighted to give them assistance."

"I am sure we must be prepared to do that," Higashi replied. "Am I correct in thinking, General Kuroki, that Major-General Ijichi will command the expeditionary force to Britain? He should become Acting Governor in the first instance. And perhaps I could persuade you, Count Furaya, to act as civil adviser to him until more permanent arrangements can be put in place."

"It seems to me that we're parcelling out the hide and horns before the prey has been caught," said Councillor Hiraoka, glumly shaking his head. "And if we do succeed in taking over the island, who is going to foot the bill? The Company, I suppose."

"I would expect that we shall find Governor Shen Fu's treasury in London well supplied; and since we are now in a state of war, we can seize their Company's assets which, as you know are very considerable." As Hiraoka's face brightened at this reminder of potential profit the Governor-General continued, "And I think we would do well not to neglect arrangements for the civil governance of the island. Admiral Katsura is right to remind us of the serious consequences that can result from any interruption in the exercise of governmental control, however brief. I am sure we shall find the native officials willing to co-operate. They will not want their wages to stop being paid."

"Admiral Katsura was also right when he spoke of taking 'nominal' possession of the island," Count Furaya observed. "The Shantungese have never had more than nominal possession themselves. Their writ doesn't run much beyond the south and east of the island, and an enclave around their factory at Edinburgh, in the north. The rest they leave to the governance of the local magnates, who spend most of their energies squabbling amongst themselves. Governor Shen Fu has, I believe been very effective in playing them off against one another without having to physically intervene. For the time being we shall need to follow his example, since I presume the number of troops available to General Ijichi will be severely limited."

"That is true," said Higashi, "but I would guess that the Shantungese Company's native regiments would be willing, once they see that the war is lost, to change paymasters. What do you think, General?"

"I agree, Your Excellency," Kuroki replied. "What they'll need, of course, will be new officers, and those are going to be in short supply – especially ones who can speak in either Shantungese or the British language. Could be an opportunity for some of our bright non-commissioned fellows to win promotion. I'll put the matter in hand without delay."

And so the Council went on discussing details of appointments and logistics while I fretted for the meeting to be over. I knew that Okada would have plenty of work for me to do as a result of the decisions that had just been made, and I wanted to get it finished before the end of the afternoon. Then I would be able to run through the sunlit streets to Count Furaya's house and see again that face which to my longing eyes would be more dazzling than any sun.

CHAPTER 11

On my way to Count Furaya's house I made a short detour to the Grote Markt, where I had several times seen a pale but pretty young native girl selling flowers. From her I bought a bunch of roses, flowers with pink petals that grow wild in the hedgerows. Their stems are studded with sharp thorns, and had I been of a poetic disposition I should, no doubt, have been thinking lofty thoughts about the contiguity of pain and pleasure underlying the alluring aspect of love. As it was, being a pragmatic young fellow, I reminded myself as I hurried along Kaasrui that I must warn Ermyntrude to take care when she handled the flowers.

The exuberance that had surged through me that morning when I heard Admiral Katsura explain the reason for her absence on my previous visit had now given way to anxiety about how she would receive the overtures I was determined to make to her. Did I have any real reason to believe that she was as eager to see me as I to see her? And, apart from giving her the flowers, how should I begin to let her know that my feelings for her went deeper than friendship? If I blurted out some conventional phrase like 'When I was far away I suddenly realized that I was in love with you' she might be totally unprepared for it.

There were several reasons why Ermyntrude might not entertain any amorous feelings towards me, I reminded myself. I was a foreigner, and one whose physical appearance she might not even find attractive. For several years she had been living in a nunnery, and even though she seemed to have abandoned the beliefs that had led her to make that choice, it was possible she might still have a preference for celibacy. She was also totally dependent on Count Furaya's generosity and goodwill, and so she might not have allowed herself to entertain the thought of any relationship that could threaten her position in his household.

But she also undoubtedly had feelings of gratitude towards me for having rescued her from Britain. I didn't want those feelings to influence her response to me now. Love and gratitude were two completely different emotions, I believed. I was old enough to have seen people try to use gratitude as blackmail to obtain something they wanted from a beneficiary, and it was a tactic that I utterly despised. I needed to find an opportunity to assure Ermyntrude that she didn't owe me anything. The only reward I needed for her rescue was to see her living in freedom.

Turning into Wolstraat, I was seized by a very different anxiety. Ermyntrude might yield to my advances out of fear. She might think I was claiming her as my rightful 'prize', and that if she refused me the Count, *in loco parentis*, might support my claim and turn her out of his house. That was a reason for which I would certainly not want her to accept me – but then I told myself she had the courage not to be intimidated. However, confronting the possibility made me realize there was another question I hadn't resolved: what was I really going to offer Ermyntrude?

I knew that I wanted more than just the stimulus of her conversation and the warm reassurance of her company. I longed to hold her close to me, and then go on to use all the skills Sophia had taught me to find out how much pleasure I was able to give her. And in that mutual discovery of joy I wanted somehow to be united with her. But would it be a union that was secret, known only to ourselves and constrained by our circumstances to a series of clandestine couplings? Or should I openly – if Okada didn't forbid it – take her as my mistress, to live with me in whatever lodgings I could afford? Or should I ask her to marry me?

The thought of marriage was so disturbing that I collided with a water-seller as I rounded the corner into Grote Godaert. He dropped the cask he was carrying but fortunately it didn't split, though he let fly a string of curses that I was happily unable to understand. Marriage was something I had never seriously thought about before. Since I was setting out for Europa to make my fortune it was assumed by my family that I would not be looking for a wife until I came home again, laden with wealth. And that might well be ten years hence.

Suddenly marriage was no longer associated in my mind with wealth or family expectations, and certainly not with going home again. If I was going to marry a native woman going back to Japan might no longer be an attractive proposition. I could hear an echo of all the judgements that were commonplace among acquaintances where I grew up when they talked about Europeans – lazy, ignorant, superstitious, dirty (they didn't have baths), perpetually smelling of mutton and dangerously inscrutable. What kind of welcome could a European wife expect?

And if I didn't go home again, did I really want to start taking responsibility now for a woman – and then maybe for children? Wasn't it too soon to be shackled by family commitments? But I *wanted* to be committed to Ermyntrude, because I wanted her to be committed to me. I didn't want to stop having new adventures, but I wanted to have someone to come home to, just as I felt I was now coming home, as I knocked on the door of Count Furaya's mansion.

Once again the door was opened by the liveried manservant, who permitted himself a small knowing smile as he glanced at the roses in my hand. "I delivered your strawberries last night when the young lady returned, sir," he said. "She appeared to be very pleased to receive them."

Remembering the advice my father had once given me on the importance of making allies among servants, I fumbled in my pocket and pressed a ten sen coin into his hand. He bowed gravely and then led me down the familiar corridor.

The expression on Ermyntrude's face when I entered the library sent a surge of hope that expelled the doubts from my mind. Her blue eyes positively sparkled with delight as she sprang up from her chair; but then, I suppose, the deeply ingrained habit of modesty intervened, for she curtsied with bowed head and said, "Welcome back from your wanderings. I am sorry I wasn't here when you called yesterday."

I presented her with the roses, remembering to warn her about the thorns. She laughed delightedly and said, "When I was a little girl I used to pick them from the hedges and I often pricked my fingers. I once picked a bunch for my cell in the nunnery, but that got me into trouble. The Prioress told me I should not be looking at flowers which were symbols of earthly passion, but instead I should be contemplating the sufferings of Our Lord on the cross."

"Are these flowers symbolic of earthly passions?" I asked.

"Oh yes. At home every flower is symbolic of something, if you give it as a gift. A rose is for love – but of course you didn't know that."

"I know it now and it makes me happy, because…" I hesitated, and I could actually feel my heart pounding in my chest. This was the moment and I had to seize it. "…because when I bought the flowers I wanted them to tell you that I love you." I said it, and time seemed to stand still as I watched her face to see what her response would be.

Her smile was pure joy. "You really wanted to tell me that? All the time while you were away I kept wondering if it might ever happen. I knew I mustn't say it to you, even though I wanted to. I couldn't believe it was ever going to happen." She laid the roses on the table and stretched out her hand, very tentatively, to touch my arm.

At her touch I instantly lost the restraint I had been imposing on myself. I stepped forward, grasped her by the shoulders and drew her close to me. Her blue eyes were sparkling with anticipation as I bent my head to kiss her. Our lips collided a little clumsily as she, at the last moment, raised her mouth to meet mine; but within a second we had repositioned them and were locked in a kiss that told me everything I wanted to know about her feelings for me.

When at last I withdrew my lips from hers her face remained upturned towards me, eyes still closed and mouth half open, awaiting my return. Once again I savoured the softness of her welcoming lips, and my fingers began to explore the line of her back through the coarse grey woollen material of her dress. As my hands pressed over the hollows of her slender waist and came to rest on the firm curves of her buttocks, hitherto concealed by the looseness of her garments, I experienced an instant erection. She could not have been aware of this, for I refrained from pressing against her, and yet, when our mouths parted once more, she said, "Where are we going to do it? Will you be able to find somewhere?"

For a moment I didn't know what she meant and stupidly asked, "Do what?"

Her cheeks reddened as she replied, "You know… make love. Isn't that what you want to do?"

I laughed with delight and kissed her cheek. "Of course it is, but I want a lot more than that. I want you to be my wife. Then we won't have to go to some secret place to love each other. Will you marry me?"

Her eyes rounded with astonishment. "You want to marry me? I didn't think you would ever want to do that. I'm only a British girl, with no family, no land – nothing to give you. You might even get into trouble."

"You mean you were ready to… make love with me even though you thought I wouldn't ever marry you?"

"Yes, I was. You must think I have no shame. The Prioress would tell me I was going straight to hell. But I don't care. I love you, and I may never get the chance to love anybody else. But would it be right for you to marry me? I haven't got anything to give you."

"You will give me love," I replied. "That's worth more than anything else. I realized that when I was away in Brunswick. What I wanted then was to have someone to come back to – someone who loved me."

"And I wanted you to come back, even though I didn't know you felt like that about me. Oh yes, I'd rather be your wife, but how could we do it? They wouldn't marry us in a church because I'm supposed to be married already – to Jesus; and of course you're a heathen. How is it done in Japan?"

"There are several different ways; but for us the important thing would be what's called a 'civil marriage', so that you would be my legal wife. It's quite a new idea. They thought of it not long before I was born. It would mean you would be protected by the law – and the Company. I'm not quite sure how we do it, but I'll find out."

She put her arms around my neck and said, "I don't really care how we do it so long as I can be with you. There's a story in the Christian holy book we call the Bible about a woman whose name was Ruth. She married the son of a widow who had come to her country in a time of famine, but the young man died and his mother was left on her own again and decided to go back to her own country. When she told her daughter-in-law she was leaving Ruth said to her: 'Wherever you go I will go, and where you stay I will stay, and your people will be my people and your god will be my god.' The story had a happy ending, because her mother-in-law eventually found her another husband, who was very kind to her, and they had a son who was an ancestor of Jesus, the Christian god.

"Anyhow, when you were away and I realized that you were the one I really loved, I told myself that if ever you showed me that you wanted me I would say to you what Ruth said. So I'm saying it now: wherever you go I will go, and wherever you stay I will stay, and your people will be my people – if they'll have me."

"That might be a problem," I said kissing her lightly on the forehead," just as I expect your people might not be very happy about having me. But we'll find our own space to live in, and we'll make our own friends. Everything is changing now. We'll be the first in a new world, not the last in an old one."

Standing on tiptoe she kissed me, and the softness of her lips on mine filled me with tenderness and passion. I wrapped my arms around her and held her close, feeling a heat in her slender body that matched the fever of my own desire. Again we kissed, and our mouths seemed to become a tunnel through which we were trying to enter one another. I felt her fingers beginning to explore the line of my back, moving down to my buttocks – and then I heard a cough.

We leapt apart and turned to face the door. Count Furaya was standing there, his face totally inscrutable. "If I may interrupt your… reunion," he said, "there are some matters of importance that I need to discuss with you in my study, young man."

I turned and made a hasty bow to Ermyntrude and, noting the look of anxiety in her eyes, mouthed a kiss to her. Then I followed the Count along the corridor to his study, to which I had never previously been admitted. He gestured to me to sit down and, to my great relief, immediately began speaking about work.

"It would seem that we are once again to be travelling companions," he said. "I have just come from a discussion with the Governor-General and Senior Factor Okada about the staff that will accompany me to London, assuming that our forces are able to take possession there without undue delay. It was agreed that you should go along with the combined functions of Latin correspondent for the Acting Governor and myself and organizer of Okada's… information network in Britain. He will, of course, explain to you what that will involve. I understand that he already has a number of agents in the island. It will be a demanding assignment but, as I am sure you can see, it will provide an early and swift advancement of your career."

"Indeed, sir, I do see that," I replied, taken aback by the rapidity with which my life was changing. "I'm very honoured to have been selected… and I shall greatly welcome the opportunity to work with you once again."

"Our last excursion together certainly proved to be profitable for you," he said. "Are you intending to make the young woman your mistress?"

Taken off guard by his question I stammered, “No… no, I’m not.” And recovering my composure I added, “I have asked her to be my wife.”

“And has she consented?”

“Yes, she has. But we had just begun to talk about it, and we… we knew we would have to… consult with you about it.”

“Indeed,” said the Count, and he stroked his chin reflectively several times before continuing. “No doubt you have thought about the implications of what you intend to do. Is it your intention, then, to make a permanent career for yourself here in Europa?”

“It is, sir. I have decided that this is where I want to live and make my future.”

“Well, there are some precedents that may encourage you,” he said. “When you were in Brunswick did you by any chance encounter Colonel Shunzo?”

“I did, sir, and a colleague told me his story. I wouldn’t aspire, perhaps, to be so… prolific, but I certainly admire his achievements.”

The Count smiled. “Indeed. And there are others, of varying rank, who appear to have found a satisfactory manner of living between two worlds. I trust that the outcome for yourself – and the young woman – will also be fortunate.”

He paused, looking thoughtful, and I murmured my thanks for his good wishes. Stroking his chin once again, he said, “As it happens, this might be an especially propitious moment for your intended union. I had, anyhow, intended to take Ermyntrude with me to Britain. Her translating skills and her intelligent appraisal of her fellow-countrymen will be extremely valuable to me – as they will also be to you in your work for Okada. Incidentally, he mentioned that you will be receiving a bonus for the services which you rendered to the Company while in Brunswick. Very timely from your point of view, I should think.” From the quizzical look that he gave me I guessed that he knew what those services had involved.

My delight at the thought of some additional cash to spend on Ermyntrude mingled with joy at the realization that I wasn’t, after all, going to be separated from her by my new responsibilities.

"It will also be to the Company's advantage, I believe, that the natives in Britain see a member of their new administration married to one of their own kind," the Count continued. "I expect some of my colleagues would not agree, but I have always taken the view that Japan will have a presence in this sub-continent for many generations to come. If it is going to be a fruitful presence it will have to be founded not just on power but on harmonious relationships with the native peoples. And many thousands of personal unions like the one on which you are about to embark will contribute to that harmony. Who knows, one of your descendants might become the first governor-general to be born in the sub-continent? Oh yes, I believe that's something that must happen if our presence here is ever to be permanent."

I could see that he was talking as much to himself as to me, but then there was an abrupt change in his manner. Looking directly at me, he enquired, "Have you thought yet about how you are going to proceed? There may not be a lot of time, if you are to arrive in London as man and wife. I take it from what you said that you want to make the relationship a legal one."

"Indeed yes, sir, but I haven't had time yet to find out what the procedure is."

"Well, I have just had an idea that might greatly simplify the process for you," he said thoughtfully, stroking his chin. "In the circumstances I imagine that traditional ceremonies of one kind of another were not going to feature largely in your plans. If that is so, perhaps you would permit me to make a suggestion."

"I should be most grateful if you would, sir," I replied.

"A couple of decades ago," he went on, continuing to stroke his chin, "those New Continent colonists who are giving us so much trouble at the moment petitioned for legislation that would give authority to commanding officers of ships on the high seas to perform legally binding marriage ceremonies. I understand their request was prompted by the exigencies of those interminable voyages to and fro across the Great Ocean. Anyhow, the legislation was duly enacted.

"Now you and your intended bride should very soon be making a voyage, albeit a short one, across the sea to Britain. I can see no reason why we could not arrange for the captain of the vessel to which we are assigned to carry out the ceremony at the time when we are on the high seas. It will not take long, and will doubtless make a welcome diversion from warlike activities for him and his crew. What do you think?"

"I think that is a splendid idea, sir. I am greatly indebted to you."

"Then we must make sure that it happens. I will talk to you again when you've been given your instructions by Senior Factor Okada. But now you must return to your British bride and tell her the news. I'm afraid we may have left her full of fear that her happiness was about to be snatched away from her."

"She may have been fearful, sir," I said, "but she's also full of courage."

CHAPTER 12

"The English name of that ruined castle is Gravesend," said Ermyntrude, pointing to the southern shore of the estuary. "The Taiwanese were allowed to build it by a king called Henry about two hundred and fifty years ago, after they'd helped him to defeat a Turkish invasion. They already had a factory at Cowes, on an island south of Britain."

We were standing on the quarterdeck of the Imperial Navy sloop *Usugumo*, in the company of Count Furaya and the newly-promoted captain, Hirose, my companion on the previous visit to Britain. It was Hirose who had performed our marriage ceremony early that morning on the second day of our voyage from Antwerp. His delight at being entrusted with the task seemed to be genuine. Afterwards the Count had paid for a round of sake to be distributed to the ship's crew, who had cheered us to the echo. The wedding breakfast, in Hirose's cabin, had been a modest affair, but that didn't bother us. We were married, and in future we would be having breakfast together every morning – on our own.

"So when did the Taiwanese move their factory into London?" I asked.

"I think that must have been about thirty years later," Ermyntrude replied. "I wish now I could remember more of the history my Uncle Edward went to so much trouble to teach me. I know the Taiwanese helped King Henry to reconquer North Britain."

"Who had taken it away from him?" asked Hirose.

"It happened when his father, who was also called Henry, won the crown from his cousin, Richard. He needed to have help from some of the European soldiers who came over here from Europa when the Turks finally got to the Channel coast. Some of them were on Richard's side; but a very powerful leader called Charles the Bold, who had been the King of Burgundy, sided with Henry and helped him to win. But Charles and his followers wanted to have their share of the land and they set up a kingdom of North Britain – all of the land north of the rivers Ribble and Tees. It eventually fell apart, with the barons all fighting each other, after Charles died, and Henry – the son – didn't have much trouble winning it back.

"But it didn't do him much good, because about twenty years later he fell out with the Taiwanese. They were much stronger by then; and they'd taken care not to let him have any guns. So they got rid of him and divided the island up among three puppet kings. Two of them were barons who had helped them defeat Henry: a man called Edward Seymour, who became King of North Britain; and John Dudley, whom they made King of West Britain. The south, which was still called England, was given to Henry's younger son, Arthur, who was sickly and feeble-minded. When he died they didn't bother to find another king, and four big barons, called the Earls of Wessex, Sussex, Mercia and Essex, were allowed to run things outside of London and Southampton – and Cornwall, of course, where the tin mines were. I think that was still the way things were, more or less, when the Shantungese drove out the Taiwanese about a hundred and fifty years ago."

Count Furaya, who had been listening to her very intently, said, "You mentioned that refugees from the Turks in Europa had helped the older Henry to win his battles. Have they often been influential in the history of the island?"

"My Uncle Edward used to describe them as 'the curse of the country'," she replied. "The first wave of them actually arrived five hundred years ago, when the Mongols overran the continent. It was because he had their help that a king called Edward was able to make the whole island into one country for the first time. They were ready to fight for him if he would allow them to take over land that was conquered; so he had a big army that he didn't have to pay, and he was able to defeat the Welsh and the Scots. And they also helped him to repel an invasion by the Mongols. I think that was exactly five hundred years ago this year. People were planning to celebrate it when I was in the nunnery. It was a specially important victory because the Mongols were heathen and might have destroyed the Church. They'd killed the Pope not long before that.

"But there was always trouble between the new barons and the old ones. My uncle said that was the main reason why the country was always divided and it was easy for people from outside, like the Taiwanese, to take over."

At that moment there was a strong gust of the south-easterly wind that had been keeping our sails filled, and an acrid smell assailed my nostrils. "I think I can smell charcoal," I exclaimed.

Hirose laughed. “That will be from the embers of the ships at Chatham,” he said. “The wind is still catching the embers, and they must be a good ten miles away.”

“Your fireships did a very effective job, then,” the Count commented. “Presumably that’s why the Shantungese garrison in London gave in so quickly.”

“Yes, Your Excellency. They knew our ships’ guns would be able to go on pounding them without interruption. It was good that we didn’t have to spend too long here, because the squadron is already well on its way to take Southampton.”

“Are you sorry not to be sailing with it?” asked Ermyntrude.

”No, there’s plenty to keep me busy here,” he replied. “I’ve been ferrying prisoners of war over to Walcheren and, of course, bringing back important people like yourselves. But very soon there should be some prizes to intercept, and that’s something we’ll all enjoy.” He grinned at the helmsman, who could overhear what he was saying.

As we rounded a huge bend in the estuary we could see the evening sun like a red ball in the clear sky directly ahead of us. “If this wind remains steady we should arrive at the Tower just before dark,” said Hirose.

“You know,” said the Count, turning to Ermyntrude, “what your uncle said about the divisions in your country making it vulnerable to conquerors from outside has made me think about this war that’s bringing us here today. It’s all about quarrels between countries thousands of miles away from here, and yet it’s going to determine how your people live for – who knows how long? – maybe the next hundred years or more. But these quarrels that we have between powerful states in East Asia keep recurring, just like the civil wars you used to have in Britain. It may well be that some day one of our wars will provide your people with an opportunity to be rid of us and start running their own affairs once more, with the old divisions long forgotten. But if that does ever happen I hope your people will have learned some lessons in the meantime, so that they can make their future better than the past.”

“What kind of lessons do you mean?” asked Ermyntrude.

“How to have a strong system of government that enjoys the support of all the people because they know they can trust it. That would be one," the Count replied. "Finding ways to settle disputes without fighting each other would be another; and so would learning how to make decisions based on reasoned argument and not on prejudice or superstition. They're lessons we haven't yet learned in East Asia, but some of us do know what the questions are, even if we haven't found the answers."

"I remember reading something in a book that was written by one of the Ancient Greeks," said Ermyntrude, wrinkling her forehead in a concentrated effort to remember. "The writer said there would be no end to the troubles of humanity until philosophers became kings in the world, or until those who are called kings and rulers truly became philosophers."

"Now that is an interesting thought," said the Count, and I could see that he looked at Ermyntrude with new respect in his eyes. "What was the name of the writer?"

"He was called Plato, Your Excellency."

"I should like to read his book. Do you have a copy?"

"No; but there is a Latin translation of it in the library at the nunnery in Rochester. It's called *Republic*."

"I can see that I may have to pay the nuns a visit," said the Count. He smiled at Ermyntrude and went on, "But I think it might be better if you didn't accompany me on that occasion, though I expect that by now they will have found someone else to take care of their library."

Surreptitiously I squeezed Ermyntrude's hand as she stood by my side. In a public place I couldn't give her any other token of affection, but I felt very proud of my clever wife. The Count proceeded to question her about the contents of the library, and it was evident that he intended to ask the nuns to sell him some of their books. I hoped that he would, because I might then have an opportunity to read them.

At last, with the light beginning to fade, we sailed into the Pool of London and could see ahead of us the grey forbidding outlines of the Tower. On the top of the high, central keep a flag was being lowered and momentarily it was caught in one of the final rays of the setting sun. On its white ground I saw the red triumphant sun-disc of Japan and felt a surge of pride I had never before experienced. On my previous visit, just three months earlier, it had been the blue dragon on the orange banner of Shantung that had floated above the great fortress.

As we drew closer we could see evidence of the recent bombardment. In particular, the nearest of the towers overlooking the riverside was virtually in ruins, and with my telescope, which I now was sharing with Ermyntrude, I could see the muzzles of two cannon pointing skyward through the rubble that now crowned its summit.

"That's the second time the tower on that position in the walls has been destroyed," said Ermyntrude, handing me back the telescope. "I can remember my father pointing it out to me, on the one occasion when he brought me to London. It was called the Taiwanese Tower. They built it to replace one that they'd knocked down when they attacked King Henry. The old one was called the Cradle Tower. I think I remember that because it seemed like a funny name to give to a fortification."

"Did the Taiwanese storm the fortress?" I asked.

"They didn't have to. King Henry was killed by a cannon-ball and the garrison surrendered."

"I should think it would be a pretty difficult place to storm," I observed. "I'm glad our fellows didn't have to do it."

When we finally got ashore darkness had fallen and there was a file of men from the Walloon Native Infantry with lighted torches to escort us, from the watergate through the Bloody Tower and across an open space to a row of Eastern-style houses just beneath the inner wall of the fortress. "Your lodgings are here," said the young Japanese lieutenant in command of the soldiers. I was disappointed to see that it wasn't my friend Takahashi. I should have liked him to meet Ermyntrude – and see for himself what a pretty nose she had.

"Since the hour is late the Governor has invited you to join him for a quick supper," the lieutenant went on.

"My companions as well?" enquired the Count.

"Yes, Your Excellency. General Ijichi particularly said, 'Ask Count Furaya to bring the married couple with him.'"

So our torch-bearing escort conducted us to the looming mass of the White Tower. There, in a partitioned space at one end of a huge room that might have been designed as a banqueting hall, we were received by Acting Governor Major-General Ijichi. He was a short, stocky man with a weather-beaten face and bristling moustache. His red tunic was unbuttoned, revealing a dingy white shirt covering his barrel chest.

When bows had been exchanged the General said, "Good to see you, Furaya. Hope you had a pleasant journey. Afraid we're still in some disorder here, tidying up after the abrupt departure of the former residents." He gave a short, barking laugh. "We'll have to make do with what we found in the larder till we get the locals reorganized. Take a seat. Food's on the table."

As we sat down at one end of a long table that could have accommodated twenty diners the General continued, "I'll not detain you long this evening, but we have a busy day ahead tomorrow. I expect you youngsters can't wait to have some time together on your own." With a glance at Ermyntrude and me which was clearly intended to be genial, he uttered another short, barking laugh. "I told my fellow to pick a room for you with a comfortable bed. Hope he found one."

"Most grateful, Your Excellency," I murmured, hoping he wasn't going to pursue that line of conversation. I need not have worried, for he immediately switched his attention to the Count.

"Have an important meeting tomorrow that I need you to attend," he said. "A couple of the local notables are coming to see me – the Earls of Sussex and Essex. I've sent for two of the others but it will take them a few days to get here. Can't remember their names."

Since the conversation was in Japanese Ermyntrude couldn't follow it, but I saw her glance up from her plate of rice and fish at the sound of the names. Remembering what she had told us earlier about the history of the southern province, I asked, "Would they be the Earls of Wessex and Mercia, Your Excellency?"

The General looked surprised and then nodded twice. "Quite right. Quite right. Thank you." He went on, "Apparently the roads over here are in an appalling condition. The Shantungese seem to have paid little attention to transport, apart from the coastal shipping. When things have settled down we'll have to do something about that.

A bit of road-building might be just what we need to get the native regiments used to working with us."

"I read somewhere that the island used to have a good network of roads when the Romans were here, more than a thousand years ago," said Count Furaya. "Do you know anything about Roman roads?" he asked Ermyntrude, speaking in Latin.

"Yes, my uncle told me about them. He said that some of them are still in use, but they lost their good surfaces a long time ago because people didn't know how to maintain them. There's one that runs near to where I grew up, joining London to Canterbury," she replied.

I could see that the General was struggling to understand what she said, and guessed that his Latin was less than fluent. "If they have good foundations we might start work on some of those roads," he said. "But hearing the young woman speak reminds me of a problem we're going to have tomorrow.

"I'm told that these fellows have some Latin, but not a great deal; and I'm a bit rusty in that language myself. They can understand Shantungese, but that's not a lot of help to us. We're going to have a problem understanding them. Any ideas?"

I thought I saw a solution. "Could I suggest, Your Excellency, that if Ermyntrude and I were present she could translate English into Latin for me and I could, if you wish, translate into Japanese for you – and the process could also be reversed."

"Good idea," said the General. Then he added, "But I wonder if involving a woman would… would seem appropriate to those fellows."

"That might be a problem," Count Furaya agreed.

Ermyntrude looked disappointed, but then her face brightened and she said, "I think we could get around that, Your Excellency. If someone could find a monk's habit for me I could pull the hood over my face and pretend to be a monk. If I lower my voice a bit like this" – her tone became convincingly gruff – " I could sound like a very young monk. Some of them do talk in a funny sing-song way – it's all that chanting they have to do."

The General laughed. "We'll do it. There's no time to arrange anything else. This town seems to be crawling with monks. We'll find a small one and relieve him of his gear for a few hours. He can have a couple of yen for his pains."

So it was agreed that Ermyntrude would undertake her first task as a translator on the following day, and she seemed to be well pleased at the prospect. Before long our frugal meal was at an end, and I had a feeling that the General was about to dismiss us with some ribald exhortation to Ermyntrude and myself. However, at that moment a lieutenant came in with a request that needed his urgent attention and he sent us on our way with only a wave of his hand.

On the way back to our quarters we were escorted by a solitary corporal bearing a lantern. At the foot of the stairway Count Furaya took his leave with a formal bow, saying gravely, "Every river starts its life as a tiny stream. I hope that the first night of your life together will be happy, but I hope, too, that succeeding days and years will see a steady swelling in the flow of happiness, so that you need never look behind you with regret." And taking a lighted candle from the stocky native servant who waited on us, he departed to his own room.

We were also given a candle to light us up the narrow stairway to a large bedroom, in which the shadows were already dancing in the flickering light of two four-stemmed candelabra. Our luggage had already been unpacked, and the sight of two nightgowns, both simple cotton garments, laid side by side on the big, native four-poster bed, instantly reawakened the anxiety I had been feeling earlier in the evening. What should I do to ensure that Ermyntrude's first experience of carnal love – for she must surely be a virgin – gave her more pleasure than pain? Could the lessons I had learnt from Sophia, whose virginity had been long forgotten, be of any help to me? After years in the nunnery how much did Ermyntrude actually know about the realities of love-making? But then she might well have learned all that she needed to know as a child among the animals on her father's estate – or would that only have served to increase her anxieties?

Those questions flashed through my mind as I closed the door behind us and placed the candle on a table by the bed. As I turned around Ermyntrude came towards me, her cheeks flushed and her eyes sparkling. "At last I don't have to wait any longer," she said. "I want to see what you look like. Can I take off your clothes? That's what married people do, isn't it?"

"Of course you can," I replied, and kissed her hungrily on her lips. Even before our mouths had separated I felt her fingers on the buckle of my belt. It didn't take long for her to remove my outer garments; and, not wanting her eyes to linger on my shabby undergarments, I rapidly stripped those off myself, while she crouched down to remove my boots. That task completed she stood up and surveyed my body. My rampant desire for her had very rapidly become apparent.

"You're beautiful," she said, stretching out her arms to touch my shoulders.

"Not really," I replied. "Just an average specimen. But I'm all yours, and I hope I'll serve your purpose."

Our mouths came together once again and I held her close to me, feeling her soft fingers beginning to explore my back. They started at my shoulders, stroked my spine, traversed my waist and firmly grasped my buttocks, while I marvelled at her lack of inhibition. It seemed that my fears had been unfounded.

Gently releasing myself from her grasp I started to undo the girdle of her grey, woollen dress. "Now I believe some real beauty is going to be revealed," I said, plucking at the garment where it clung to her hips, so that I could pull it up. She raised her arms to help me take it over head. Underneath it a loose cotton shift concealed the contours of her body, and I wasted no time in making it follow the dress.

In the candlelight her pale skin had the sheen of satin, and the curves of her body were even more beautiful than I had expected. Her waist was tiny, and her small breasts stood firm and proud to greet my eager lips. When I kissed them each in turn she exhaled a sigh of satisfaction, and when my lips began to tease her nipples she uttered a soft moan.

I picked her up, delighting in the softness of her flesh against my own, and carried her to the great bed. On that warm summer night we had no need of the heavy coverlet. Because of Ermyntrude's apparent eagerness our first coupling wasn't long delayed. The loud cry with which she acknowledged penetration was more redolent of triumph than of pain. (Afterwards she told me that the pain, while expected, had been only momentary.)

Ermyntrude's subsequent delight in every new discovery reminded me how much I owed to Sophia for all she had enabled me to learn. And when we finally lay side by side, exhausted but content, the candles having long since guttered out, I remembered Count Furaya's simile of the swelling river. What he had said about the steady increase in our happiness the longer we lived together would, I hoped, turn out to be true. But I also reflected that explorers seeking for the source of some mighty river must experience a very special joy when they finally discover it, a joy that will remain with them for the rest of their lives. I looked down at Ermyntrude's face, already peaceful in sleep, and very gently kissed her lips.

THE END

If you have enjoyed *A Casual Conquest* you can now read the sequel, a story that happens two centuries later. Following are the opening pages of

Misrule Britannia

Available from www.lulu.com and www.amazon.co.uk

(ISBN 978-1-84753-968-7)

CHAPTER 1

The tip of my ballpoint skidded across the page as, for the hundredth time, the train jolted to a standstill. (It was in the days before laptops, when one computer needed a small room to accommodate it.) Smoke from the labouring locomotive drifted past the carriage window, and I rubbed the glass with the heel of my hand to clear it of condensation. I could see the menacing shapes of howitzers squatting under their tarpaulins on the flat-cars of a train halted on the parallel track, and I wondered if they might be the guns manned by the five young officers facing me across the compartment – all artillerymen by their badges.

My newspaper's local correspondent had been very lucky – or had pulled some useful strings – to get me a seat on this northbound train, with half of the army moving to the same destination. He was a lecturer at the university in the capital city, who wrote an occasional piece for my paper when there was anything worth reporting from this normally very un-newsworthy ex-colonial territory. But now that the place seemed to be on the verge of civil war the Foreign Editor had sent me ten thousand miles to cover it at first hand. There's nothing like a spot of violence to justify the price of an air fare.

I'd spent the previous evening getting a hurried briefing from the local stringer on this, to me, totally unfamiliar country. Until twenty-four hours before it had meant little more than a half-remembered school geography lesson: chief exports – wool, coal and iron-ore, or was it fish? I recalled a textbook picture of a huge temple with spires and painted windows and elaborate stone carvings. Now the natives were going to start killing each other, largely because of the oil that one of our companies had discovered beneath their territorial waters. (I'd have to be careful not to use that word "natives" in my copy. It had gone out of favour because of the racist connotations given to it by the semi-literate.)

Once again the train jolted into motion and a young officer who had been dozing lurched forward, awakening just in time to prevent himself from sliding to the floor. His comrades laughed at his discomfiture in the loud, raucous manner of their country. I wished that I could understand what they were saying, since their conversation might have provided some "human interest" for my report, and I was well aware that the readers would appreciate a little light relief to the indigestible details of politicians with unpronounceable names. Still, they'd have to have those details if they were going to follow what was happening over the next few days.

I peered out at the passing countryside with renewed interest, now that we'd left behind the depressing shanty towns that clustered around the capital city. They made it look like every other developing country I'd visited – except that, somehow, the huts made of plywood boxes with palm-leaf roofs I'd seen in Pelembang didn't depress me as much as these hovels of tarred timber and corrugated iron rusting in the cold northern rain. But now that we were out among the hills and trees, speeding through a patchwork of tiny cultivated fields, the alien landscape seemed more welcoming in spite of the drizzle.

I turned my attention back to the notebook resting on my knee and began to write:

> *Last night the National Assembly met in the capital, London, to discuss the rapidly worsening crisis. Prime Minister John Serjeant faced fierce criticism from the opposition People's Democratic Party for his handling of the situation in Scotland, the disaffected northern province. He was even accused by veteran leader of the independence movement and founder of his own party, Edward Shrub, of inflaming the army mutiny which has brought this country to the verge of civil war.*
>
> *Four days ago Serjeant ordered the arrest of the newly-emerged leader of the break-away Scottish Covenant League, Andrew Knox, for allegedly trying to incite the garrison in Edinburgh, the provincial capital, to mutiny. A mob rescued Knox from the city's ancient Tolbooth Prison, and when the garrison, men of a Scottish regiment, were ordered to disperse the rioters they refused to leave their barracks in the castle.*
>
> *Immediately Serjeant ordered two other regiments to Edinburgh, to disarm the mutineers, one from the north of England (largest province of the British Republic) and the other from the north of Scotland. The latter regiment is composed mainly of highlanders recruited from remote mountain regions, who speak a different language from the men in Edinburgh and were apparently expected to have little sympathy with them.*

However, Prime Minister Serjeant seems to have made the double mistake of doubting their reliability while depending on their loyalty. He sent an English Lieutenant-Colonel from London by plane to take command of the operation; but the Scottish colonel was affronted by this slight to his rank and refused to accept the Englishman's orders. So the regiment marched into Edinburgh and joined forces with the mutineers. When the English regiment came up next day it prudently decided to dig in on the outskirts of the city and await reinforcements.

In the Assembly yesterday Opposition leader Mark Gowrie urged restraint in the interests of national unity. He proposed that the mutinous troops should be offered an amnesty, and that a constitutional conference should be arranged to discuss a federal solution. But this proposal was rejected outright by the Prime Minister.

Mr. Serjeant argued that the crisis was all the work of a handful of militants who represented nobody but themselves. His government had been democratically elected to govern, and that was what it intended to do. Whatever force might be needed to disarm the mutineers would be used, and law and order would be restored in the Scottish province.

The Prime Minister received strong support from Anne Cobbleigh, leader of the Christian Heritage Party, a minority group in the governing coalition. There are known to be strong Buddhist elements in the Scottish break-away movement (Japanese missionary influence was strong in Scotland) and the CHP was responsible for recent legislation banning non-Christians from government jobs.

When the Assembly voted in the early hours of this morning the CHP combined with Mr. Serjeant's British People's League to overwhelm the Opposition. With all but two of the fourteen members of the moderate Scottish People's League voting with the government, the issue was never really in doubt.

So now it looks as if the gun, which has been absent from politics in Britain since the granting of independence by Japan eleven years ago, will decide the outcome. Units based in the southern provinces of England and Wales constitute the overwhelming majority of the armed forces, but because of the country's poor communications network it may be several days before they can all reach the northern town of Newcastle upon Tyne, where a punitive expeditionary force is being assembled.

The rain clouds had begun to drift away, and through the window I caught a glimpse of a mellow stone tower brooding over a cluster of little houses. I presumed it must be a Christian temple, and its photogenic qualities prompted me to wonder whether a photographer would be waiting for me in Newcastle, as promised.

Our British correspondent, John Marlowe, had arranged for me to be met in Newcastle by a man who would act as guide, interpreter and driver for the rest of the journey.

"If anything needs to be fixed, Bernie will fix it," he'd said.

I hoped he was right. One of the things that Bernie was going to arrange was a local photographer to accompany us to the battlefield – or whatever it was that lay ahead. I wasn't sure if any of the international news agencies had put a photographer in yet, and it would be quite a coup if the *Nagoya Guardian* could get some exclusive pictures.

The train began to slow down again and one of the soldiers stood up and opened the window to look out. A wisp of smoke from the engine drifted in and the smell took me straight back to my childhood and the days when we still had steam trains in Japan. The town where I grew up was a railway junction, and I often walked to the bottom of the road to watch the Asahikawa express go thundering across the bridge, its mantle of smoke swirling behind it and – if the wind was from the south – filling my nostrils with the acrid, exciting smell of travel to distant places. Petrol fumes have never had the same effect on me.

It was evening and the light had almost gone when we finally clanked and creaked our way into the station at Newcastle. I climbed down stiffly on to the platform, my muscles cramped from sitting so long in one position. There were few civilians around, apart from the railway staff in their Eastern-style uniforms. I picked my way through piles of kitbags towards the entrance hall, which was built in the rather flamboyant style that characterized Japanese architecture about seventy years ago, when we were still confident of our imperial destiny.

Suddenly I saw my own name, printed in red letters on a large sheet of white paper. The paper was being held aloft by a stocky man with a round, close-cropped head of black hair and a red face that was puckered with intense concentration as he scanned the approaching stream of travellers. The moment I turned in his direction he noticed me and began to walk towards me.

"Mr. Hashimoto?" he asked.

"Yes," I replied. "And you will be Bernie Samuel?"

He bowed. "The same, in person. Have a good journey then?" His pronunciation of Japanese was good, but his voice had a curious, nasal intonation. He took my suitcase and I followed him out into the station forecourt, which was crammed with military trucks.

"We're parked around the corner," said Bernie. "Never get out through that lot." I followed him to a side street where we found a dirty, but fairly new Toyota Rough Rider, on the windscreen of which was a hand-printed label in red lettering which said (in English) "International Press".

"Jump in," said Bernie, opening the door and heaving my suitcase into the back. "We haven't far to go. I've booked you into the Kyoto Hotel. It's smaller than the Republic, but the food's better."

On the short journey he asked me a few polite but searching questions about myself – where I came from, what I did, how much I earned. The answers seemed to satisfy him, for he grinned at me as we got out of the Rough Rider and said, "You leave it to me, captain. We'll find the big news, wherever it is."

I enquired about the photographer. He would be coming up from York, the regional capital, in the morning, said Bernie. It had been a bit difficult to find one, since there was only a single newspaper in the North and its man was fully occupied. But he'd been on to an agency that did commercial work – advertisements, tourist brochures, that kind of thing – and they'd promised to send their best cameraman. Bernie was fairly certain they had only two, but he'd seen some of their work and it was good. I was very doubtful. Press photography was a lot different, and even more so under war conditions. Maybe it hadn't been such a good idea after all.

I finished writing my story before going to bed. It would be time enough to send it off in the morning. That was one advantage of reporting from a place that was nine hours behind Otsu Mean Time.

The rain had cleared next morning and there were even a few weak shafts of sunlight flickering between the scurrying grey clouds when I looked through the window at breakfast. Bernie had been up before me, getting petrol. There was likely to be a shortage, with all the military vehicles around, he said.

We were just finishing breakfast when a tall girl in a long, black, woollen cloak walked into the dining-room. There were, I suppose, a dozen people in the room and every one of them must have looked in her direction the moment she crossed the threshold.

She was a little above average height for a European woman, and a halo of glistening black curls gave her added stature. But it was her face that immediately drew my eyes – and everyone else's. She wasn't beautiful in any of the conventional patterns of feminine beauty, either Eastern or Western. Her face was a shade long, perhaps, and her mouth was wide and full, but the proportions were pleasing. It was her eyes, however, that made the face so compelling. They were widely spaced, large and dark, fringed with long lashes and flashing with vitality.

Her skin was not the usual Western blend of pink and white, or grey. It was a light, creamy brown in colour. And her nose, now that I looked at it, was decidedly flat. I guessed that she was no more than part British – almost certainly an Aiseuropean.

The girl came towards our table and I rose to greet her. She smiled, with so much warmth and sweetness and – so it seemed to me – sincerity that I felt I had just been awarded a prize.

"Mr. Hashimoto?" she asked, and, looking at Bernie, "Mr. Samuel?"

"Yes," I replied, wondering what her business with me could be.

"I'm Miranda Medway," she said. "I've come from Northern Visual Services, to do the photographs for you."

For a moment I stared at her, stupidly, and I saw the sparkle in her eyes begin to fade. She seemed to know what I was thinking. A woman press photographer in Japan would have been unusual, but here, in a developing country, where 'women's rights' were a novelty introduced only in the past decade, the idea would never have occurred to me.

"You realize this could be very dangerous?" I asked. "We're going to keep right up close to the fighting, if there is any."

Her dark brown eyes looked at me very seriously. "I can only die once – the same as you," she said. I laughed, and the sparkle came back into her eyes.

"Please sit down," I said. "Have you had breakfast yet?"

"I don't usually eat breakfast," she replied, "but I'd love a cup of tea."

She undid the clasp at her neck and slipped off the long cloak, revealing the kind of figure that used to haunt my adolescent daydreams. Her measurements would not have won an Eastern beauty contest, but in my eyes they were perfection. Her breasts were big and firm beneath her white Eastern-style sweater, and when she turned to lay her cloak over a chair I caught my breath at the symmetry of the line from waist to thigh revealed in the swirl of her calf-length black skirt.

I know that the sudden change in my attitude would have merited the scorn of *Nagoya Guardian* readers, but I felt no guilt on that score. 'To be stirred by a woman's beauty is to pay tribute to the fountainhead of all aesthetic feelings', says Pun Poo in his *Contemplations.* And a hundred years later Wang and a score of other psychologists confirmed his intuitive belief that all appreciation of beauty has its source in human beings' primal responses to the sexually attractive characteristics of their mates. If I hadn't been influenced by this woman's face and figure it would have been a denial of her humanity as well as my own. I wouldn't pretend that those were precisely the thoughts that passed through my mind as I watched Miranda take her seat at the table that morning, but I think there was probably a split-second rehearsal of the argument as I made a cerebral gear change.

“We may have to rough it fairly often on the road. You’re quite sure you don’t mind that?” I asked, hoping that her answer would be “no” – and it was. Of course, she had never been on an assignment quite like this before, she said. But she had once taken pictures of an air crash in the Pennines that were used in *The Times of Europa.*

“How did you get into the picture-taking business, then?” asked Bernie. “A bit unusual for a girl, isn’t it?”

“Yes, I know,” she answered, smiling at him in a way that unaccountably made me feel jealous. “I think they took me on because they were too surprised to say ‘no’. It started really when my uncle gave me a camera for Christmas.” (Christmas, I learnt later, is a Christian festival which is marked by the exchange of gifts.) “Then I had a chance to go on a photography course that was starting at the London Technical College just when I was leaving school. Needless to say, everybody predicted that I would never get a job, but I did.” She looked at me with a candour that would have disarmed any doubting prospective employer.

“You got all your gear outside, then?” asked Bernie. She nodded enthusiastically. “Right, then. We’re ready to go.” It was clear that any misgivings he might have had had vanished – although there was no real reason why they should have.

I decided that we had better try to find the military headquarters as soon as possible, and discover – if anyone would tell us – when the army was likely to be ready to move. It would be a good idea, I thought, to get into Scotland ahead of them and observe their advance, provided I didn’t cut myself off for too long from communications. There wouldn’t be much point in having a sensational story if I couldn’t get to a telephone or a telex that was working, and it was unlikely that there would be many of those between Newcastle and Edinburgh.

It was late that evening before I was able to find anyone willing to talk to me at the headquarters, which was in the old Shantungese fortress (built on the site of a more ancient castle). And even then I was able to learn little, except that it would be “some days” before the deployment would be complete. Bernie’s information, from less official sources, was that two regiments, the East Anglian Rifles and the London Regiment, had not even begun to move north yet, and that there was a serious shortage of ammunition of practically all calibres.

Miranda had had no difficulty in taking pictures of the troops during the day. Her main problem had been to avoid the attempts of some of them to become more closely acquainted with her. But there were no real difficulties, for the men were good-humoured and in an almost festive mood.

I had some misgivings, however, about what might happen if we ever found ourselves in the aftermath of battle. When passions were let loose in the presence of death would the restraints of civilization still operate (perhaps 'civilization' was the wrong word to use, since these people had their own, quite ancient, civilization) or would more primitive patterns of behaviour take over? There had been many occasions when it had happened among East Asian soldiers, even in this century. However, I put the problem out of my mind. Everybody seemed to agree that there wasn't going to be a real battle.

The three of us sat in my bedroom that evening and reviewed the situation. If our information was accurate there would be no advance tomorrow, or possibly even on the next day. There was no story to be found sitting around here, and I was in favour of making a reconnaissance into Scotland. Miranda was enthusiastic about the idea, but Bernie feared that we might lose contact with the army if it were to move off suddenly.

"Supposing they decide to move across to Carlisle and strike up from there, to take the hairylegs by surprise?" he asked.

I looked at the map. "That's not very likely," I said. "There's no railway. They couldn't move the whole force quickly without using the railway."

Bernie put his neat, round head on one side and ran his fingers rapidly through his short hair in a kind of scrabbling movement. "Could be right, captain. They'd never get the tanks across the Pennines."

So we decided to head for Scotland the following day. The road was good, Bernie said (it had been built by the Japanese Army in the last century) and we should be across the Border in less than two hours. We planned to leave early in the morning, but already Bernie seemed restless to be off, and he decided to go and give the car a final check.

Also by Derek Walker (distribution at www.lulu.com and www.amazon.com)

MISRULE BRITANNIA

A journalist sent to cover a civil war in a former colony is plunged into the conflicts and corruption of an underdeveloped country. While the war escalates he falls in love with the woman of mixed race assigned to be his photographer. And when he gets close to the charismatic rebel leader he sees how personality can influence politics. The story sounds familiar, but the ex-colony is Britain and the journalist is Japanese – in an 'alternative history' scenario where eastern Asia takes on the historical role of western Europe. Looking at a world stage on which the actors have changed costumes may give the reader a new perspective on real events in recent decades. The pains and pleasures of the individual characters, however, could happen at any time, in any place.

SENSE AND SENSUALITY

When Fatima, an asylum-seeker from Kazakhstan, meets Duncan Crauford she asks him to give her a bird's eye view of the history of Western civilization, to help her become British. Their quest takes them to the British Museum, the National Gallery and other sources of 'visual aids' in London. Meanwhile, Duncan, who is secretary-general of an international think-tank, is working with Paula, a Ugandan academic, on an analysis of the UN's failure to prevent genocide in Darfur. And his erotic friendship with Helen, a sensual university lecturer, is continuing even though she has decided to look for a husband, and thinks he isn't husband material. Her rejection makes him realize that he, too, is urgently in need of someone to share his bed; but he wonders what kind of woman could possibly be interested in a battle-scarred veteran like himself.

FOND DELUSIONS

In his final year at grammar school in Northern Ireland David Hunter's ambition is to work for peace in a world where the hydrogen bomb has just been invented. He wins a scholarship to the London School of Economics, and falls in love with a beautiful classmate. But when his love affair fails he joins the Foreign Legion, and takes part in the invasion of Suez. Returning injured to London he has an unexpected encounter that gives him new hope and a better understanding of the past.

FAKING NEWS

When a minor news item on Radio 4 prompts Adam Turnbull to phone a friend he unwittingly takes the first step towards involvement in an international crisis. The action takes place a few years into the future, when Britain has a coalition government but underlying trends in politics and the media show few signs of change. When Adam, an academic specialist in Balkan Studies, is sucked into ethnic cleansing, kidnapping and diplomatic deception he witnesses ways in which political, religious and NGO groups manipulate the media and are manipulated by them. His unwitting involvement in public events also brings him into intimate contact with two attractive young women.

www.ingramcontent.com/pod-product-compliance
Ingram Content Group UK Ltd.
Pitfield, Milton Keynes, MK11 3LW, UK
UKHW040602210726
13854UKWH00008B/1763

9 781409 203407